The Fate of Her Dragon

Dragon Guard Series #10

By

Julia Mills

There Are No Coincidences.

The Universe Does Not Make Mistakes.

Fate Will Not Be Denied.

Copyright © 2015 Julia Mills

All Rights Reserved. This book or any portion thereof may not be reproduced or used in any manner whatsoever without the express written permission of the author except for the use of brief quotations in a book review.

DISCLAIMER: This is a work of fiction. Names, characters, businesses, places, events, and incidents are either the product of the author's imagination or used in a fictional manner. Any resemblance to actual persons, living or dead, or actual events is purely coincidental.

NOTICE: This is an adult erotic paranormal romance with love scenes and mature situations. It is only intended for adult readers over the age of 18.

Edited by Lisa Miller, Angel Editing Services

Cover Designed by Linda Boulanger with Tell Tale Book Covers

Cover Model Grigoris Drakakis

Formatted by Charlene Bauer with Wickedly Bold Creations

DEDICATION

Dare to Dream! Find the Strength to Act! Never Look Back!

Thank you, God.

To my girls, Liz and Em, I Love You. Every day, every way, always.

To Charlene, Your support is just amazing! This one's for you!

Also by Julia Mills

~~*~*~*~*~*

The Dragon Guard Series

Her Dragon to Slay, Dragon Guard Series #1

Her Dragon's Fire, Dragon Guard Series #2

Haunted by Her Dragon, Dragon Guard Series #3

For the Love of Her Dragon, Dragon Guard Series #4

Saved by Her Dragon, Dragon Guard #5

Only for Her Dragon, Dragon Guard #6

Fighting for Her Dragon, Dragon Guard #7

Her Dragon's Heart, Dragon Guard #8

Her Dragon's Soul, Dragon Guard #9

Her Love, Her Dragon: The Saga Begins, A Dragon Guard Prequel

*****

The 'Not-Quite' Love Story Series

Vidalia: A 'Not-Quite Vampire Love Story

Phoebe" A 'Not-Quite' Phoenix Love Story

THE FATE OF HER DRAGON

Index of the Words from the Original Language of the Dragon Kin

Draoi	Wizard
Drake	Male Dragon
Mo chroi'	My Heart
Mo ghra'	My Love
Ta' mo chroi istigh ionat	My Heart is Within You
Mo maite	Mate
Ceann beag	Little One
Mhu'chadh	Extinguish
Mo cheann a'lainn	My Beautiful One

A bheith imithe Demon	Be Gone Demon
Se'alaithe	Sealed
Solas	Light
Ara is go dti' itreann	Return to Hell
Riamh ar ais	Never Return

Chapter One

She was close… so very close. Her mind brushed against his, filling his dark, dank world with light and hope for the first time in almost a century. She exhilarated his broken spirit, mended his wounded soul, and warmed his cold, ruthless heart. Without thought, he'd spoken directly into her mind. Recognition arced between them. He willed her to respond, begging with his voice that she give him some sign—but she'd stayed silent. Her name became his mantra, the one thing keeping him sane.

Alicia…

This beautiful creature who smelled of sunshine and daffodils was to be his savior. She would be his life. She was the one the Universe had created for him. Not Heaven nor Hell nor the prison around him could keep them apart. He *knew* she would find him. Felt it in the depths of his soul. His mate possessed an inner strength that rivaled his own. She was a warrior. A woman worthy of a man like him. And she was magical… *powerful*, filled with a white magic that could overpower the evil keeping him prisoner.

Drawing on his incredible strength and years of training, the Guardsman gave one final call before collapsing from exhaustion. His body ached from exertion. His head felt as if it might explode from the constant barrage of black magic. The silver lined box buried deep in the ground, surrounded by rock and black magic, had eaten away at his strength every day of his confinement. Only his iron will and incredible healing powers had kept him alive; of course, that's what the evil wizard had counted on. The bastard knew Drago would be forced to lay helpless, trapped underground while the kin he'd spent his life protecting were destroyed.

There had been times throughout the years when the earth had shifted and Drago had been able to feel the presence of other dragons. Not those of his Force but others, some descended from the very men he'd fought beside. His dragon had come to life, snarling to make contact, but the recognition had been so brief there was no chance to call out.

Day after day, week after week, year after year, the Guardsman's frustration grew—until he was sure he'd go mad. The only thing keeping him sane was the search for his brethren. He called and called through the mindspeak of their kin, both as a group and then testing each unique link he held with the men who'd pledged their fealty to him as their Commander. Every call was answered with dead, dark silence. The Guardsman prayed his brethren lived. Was sure he would've felt their deaths, but after so much time of silence, Drago feared the worst. He searched as far as his dark magic drenched preternatural senses would allow and found nothing but the dirt around him. Even the creatures that should've inhabited the ground had been scared away by the wizard's evil spells.

Every day Drago promised himself and those whom he'd sworn to protect that he would escape his prison and dole out justice for what had been done to him and his men. All involved would pay. They would know his wrath—the wrath that kept him alive. Hate and plans of revenge had been his only company, the one reason he drew his next breath. His need for vengeance was his daily nourishment. He planned every last detail of the deaths of the wizards who had imprisoned him.

The bastards believed they were smarter than the great Dragon Guard Assassin. Had believed that attacking him from afar with their dark magic potions and sleight of hand while he was in his healing sleep would fool him, but he knew who they were. Prayed they still drew breath so that he might rob them of it. He wanted nothing more than to watch their blood soak the ground as his sword removed their heads from their bodies. But all of that was before Alicia…

Fighting to remain conscious, Drago pictured the beautiful redhead with sparkling blue eyes and a smile that made his nearly dead heart sing. When he'd touched her mind, everything had become so clear for the first time in such a very long time. He could see her long red curls glistening in the sunlight, the unmistakable twinkle of mischief in her eyes as she laughed, and the goodness shining from her heart. He dreamed of kissing each little freckle that dotted the bridge of her nose and apples of her cheeks. His hands, shackled at his sides by silver chains, ached to touch her peaches and cream complexion that looked to be softer than silk.

She was tall and curvy, just like a woman should be. As his mind stayed connected to hers, he could see her insecurities and prayed for the day he could assure his beautiful Alicia that she was perfect in every way. His heart nearly broke as their connection weakened and finally severed. He knew it was his waning strength and once again cursed the wizards responsible for his current state.

Thinking over the last few days as he rested in his tomb, Drago smiled as he remembered feeling the power of the *Dorcha* disrupted by the dragons. It had been that disturbance which had shifted the earth around his tomb, making communication with his mate possible. Now it was up to him. He had to stay alert, had to keep calling, had to make sure she found him. He needed her more than he needed his next breath. Not only was she is way out, she was the only person in all the world that could save his soul.

The words his longtime friend and mentor, Maddox, had spoken just before he and his men had embarked on their last mission floated through his mind, just as they had every day for the last hundred years. *"Take care, my friend. This mission is unlike any other. The wizards you seek are more powerful. They are cunning. It is their evil that darkens the skies."*

"Never met a wizard the lads and I couldn't beat. I earned the name 'The Assassin' ya' know? And today will not rob me of that title."

Unlike all the other times, Maddox hadn't laughed, only shook his head. *"Assassin or not, keep your wits about you."*

A cold chill had skittered down Drago's back as he'd called forth his dragon and taken to the skies. The old man always had an eerie sense of premonition, but was also a worrywart, so the Assassin and his Force had flown straight toward the enemy without a second thought to Maddox's words of warning. They defeated every evil practitioner and hunter who stood against their kin. The ground at their feet was drenched with the blood of their enemies. They'd gone into their healing sleep that night around their fire with a sense of pride and purpose.

But Fate always got her pound of flesh. Drago had awoken to the sounds of chanting and the scent of putrid herbs. Unable to open his eyes, he'd reached out with his other senses, only to find them damped by the unmistakable stench of black magic. Fighting the darkness with all the strength he had, the Guardsman reached out to his brethren, but found they too had been caught in the snare of evil magic.

Turning his focus back to the enchantment holding them all hostage, the Guardsman pushed his pure white dragon magic into the oily tendrils of the offending curse. His beast lent his strength to the fight, chuffing and blowing smoke as they fought. For several long, tense seconds he was sure he'd made headway, only to hear a menacing chuckle in his mind.

"You think to outwit me, Assassin?" The maniacal laughter made the hairs on the back of Drago's neck stand on end. *"You are no match for the Darkness that will rule the earth. Dragon kin will be destroyed and we will be victorious. Enjoy the rest of your very long life knowing I won. I beat the great Drago MacLendon."* The wizard's cackle echoed through Drago's consciousness.

He knew that voice. Had felt its slimy resonance before, but no matter how hard he tried to remember, Drago came up empty handed. It was a memory just out of his reach. He once again cursed the black magic flooding his system and fought to stay conscious. Hoisted off the ground by several sets of cold, skeletal hands, the Guardsman was unceremoniously thrown over the saddle of what he recognized by scent as his own horse. The horn of the saddle struck his ribs as he felt the bones crack, but still he struggled to gain control. Using his mental connection to the animal, Drago tried to will his trusty steed to run, but just as the wizards controlled him and his men, they also controlled his beloved horse.

The same voice that had invaded his thoughts now spoke aloud. "Take the Assassin to his new home." The wizard spoke with confidence. "Make sure he is secure. I'll be along as soon as I've taken care of the others. I want to seal the *mighty Guardsman* away myself." Once again the air filled with evil laughter as Drago ached to rip the limbs from his captor's body.

Slipping in and out of consciousness, Drago tried to map the twists and turns of his painful horseback ride as he traveled for what seemed like hours, but it was useless. He had no idea where he was being taken and was helpless to change the situation. Anger unlike any he'd ever known flooded his system. His dragon roared in his head at the injustice of their situation. But in the end, both man and beast were left to the whims of the black magic practitioners. Just as it felt as if all hope was lost, the scent of briny sea air filled the Guardsman's senses.

It was the same scent that had reached him the first time he'd felt Alicia's presence. Just the thought of his mate renewed Drago's belief that she and she alone could save him. Drawing upon years of training, both man and dragon called to their mate.

"*Alicia, mo chroi, please come to me.*"

"*Dammit man, I'm trying. I've been trying. I can hear you all hours of the day and night. I answer and you ignore. I search and find nothing. My heart is breaking and I have no clue why. I follow your voice and end up in front of a big ass boulder. It's been so long since I had a full night's sleep, I'm beginning to look like a zombie, but still you call and I come running. Hell, I don't even know who you are.*"

"*I am Drago.*"

"*What the…*" Alicia yelped. Several tense seconds later she whispered, "*What did you say?*"

"*I said, my name is Drago.*" He pushed confidence and warmth through their link, hoping to calm the turmoil he felt brewing within his mate.

Heartbeat after heartbeat, he willed Alicia to speak, to say something… *anything*. Just as gave up and was ready to call to her again, she asked, *"You're a real person? Not a figment of my imagination?"*

Chuckling, he quickly answered, "*Yes,* mo chroi' *I am real and I am sorry for your sleepless nights, but you are my only hope.*"

Confusion flooded their bond as Alicia asked, *"Your only hope for what?"*

"*To escape the prison I have been in for nearly a hundred years.*" Drago feared he'd given his lovely mate too much information too soon when his proclamation was met with deafening silence. He prayed she could feel their connection, could sense the honesty in his words and would do what needed to be done to free him. The next few moments would be crucial. Either Alicia would save him or leave him to rot away in his deep, dark prison.

Thankfully, her curiosity won over the fear he could feel resonating within her. *"Did you say a hundred years?"* Skepticism colored her words.

"Yes, I was imprisoned nearly a hundred years ago by a coven of black magic wizards known as the Dorcha.*"*

At the mention of his greatest enemy, Drago felt Alicia pull back as a wave of confusion and anger rushed over her. She quickly responded, her tone sharp and demanding. *"The* Dorcha *did this to you? Was Cleland involved?"*

"I don't know this Cleland you speak of, but I do know the Grand Draoi and his followers locked me in this God forsaken hole nearly a hundred years ago and you are my only hope of escape."

"Why would they do that? What are you, a rival wizard?"

He heard the suspicion in her voice and wondered how much to tell her then opted for the truth; it had always served him well. Alicia was magical and living near the dragons from what he'd been able to ascertain during the recent shifts in the earth, so it stood to reason she was aware of their existence and wouldn't be completely taken off guard by his next words. *"I am a Dragon Guardsman from the Golden Fire Clan. My name is Drago. I am… or, I was the Commander of the MacLendon Force. My brethren and I were captured by the* Dorcha *and hidden away as part of their plan to destroy dragon kin. Until recently, I was unable to communicate with anyone, but there was a disturbance in the black magic holding me captive and I immediately felt your presence. That is…"*

"That is when you started to slowly drive me insane." Alicia cut off his next words and began peppering him with questions. *"If you are a dragon then why communicate with me and not one of the hundred or so Guardsmen running around the countryside? And did you say MacLendon? As in Rayne MacLendon? I know*

someone said he didn't have any relatives still alive, so how can that be? And where are your men? You said the Dorcha captured them too but I can only feel your presence—and by the way, if my witchy radar is right, you're buried far underground. And that leads to me ask... how in all that is holy do you expect me to get you out of there? You said I'm your only hope... what exactly do you expect me to do? That is assuming I believe one word you're telling me."

She paused to take a breath and Drago jumped in. *"You are the only one I can communicate with. Our bond is strong because of your magic. Don't you think I tried to call out to another Guardsman? Of course, I did, but no one can hear me except you. And you know I am telling the truth. Look inside yourself, you can feel it. If you didn't you wouldn't have come all those times and you most assuredly wouldn't still be talking to me. You are a smart, intuitive woman, Alicia. You know I'm telling you the absolute truth, just as sure as you know we are mates."*

"We are what?!" Alicia sputtered just as their connection became silent.

Drago reached out with all his senses and then chuckled to himself, *"Well, bullocks, my mate has fainted."*

Chapter Two

Alicia followed the soothing tune of a low baritone hum back to consciousness. The melody seemed familiar, almost haunting, but it was the way the man's voice ignited all her senses, waking up every nerve with gentle kisses of sound that made her sigh and stretch like a kitten in the sunshine. She had a few minutes of blessed serenity before the glaring light of reality came rushing back. Jerking upright, the young witch shook her head and squinted against the rising sun. The last thing she remembered was talking to the man that had nearly driven her crazy for the last few weeks before her world had faded to black.

I can't believe I fainted. I never faint. Must've been from the lack of sleep, or…

"Did you say you think I'm your mate?" She demanded, immediately irritated when her question was met with male chuckling.

"I did."

"Well, you're wrong. I mean, you have to be wrong. It just isn't possible. And if you are making it up just so I'll help you out of whatever the Dorcha *has done to you then let me make it clear that I was going to help you anyway. I…"*

"Alicia…" Drago said her name with such command she stopped immediately, waiting for him to speak. It took several seconds but when he began again, his tone had softened. *"Let me ask you a question. Why is it that you are the only one I can communicate with even though there are other Guardsman around?"*

Not willing to admit anything, the young witch scoffed, *"I don't know… proximity?"*

Again, he chuckled, and she wished he were standing right in front of her so she could punch him in the nose. *"But did you not hear me when you were sleeping… in your home?"*

"Yes, but…"

"And were you not compelled to help me?"

"Yes, but…"

"Were you not drawn to the spot where you now stand over and over again?"

"Yes, but…

"Do you not feel our connection deep within your soul?"

"Yes, but…"

"Do you…"

"WILL YOU STOP INTERRUPTING ME?!" Alicia knew she was screaming, but Drago's incessant questioning was hitting too close to things she didn't want to think about.

Taking a long, deep breath, Alicia paced back and forth in front of the huge boulder separating her from Drago. *"Okay, I admit, I was drawn to this place. I admit I can hear you and it's obvious none of the dragons can, but there has to be a logical explanation that does* not *lead to us being mates. Right now, we need to focus on getting you out of there and I'm gonna need some serious muscle to help move this big ass rock."*

Her comments were met with silence. She was just about to ask if he was still there when he finally spoke. *"I agree to table our discussion of being mates until I am free, but do not think I will forget."*

Alicia wanted to argue, wanted to tell him that a hundred years in a hole in the ground surrounded by silver had left him a brick shy of a load—but she couldn't. There was no denying their connection. No denying what she felt just from the touch of his mind. This man was her future but there was no way she was admitting that to him, not until she could look him in the eye and make sure everything he was telling her was the truth. It was clear what she had to do.

"All right, whatever, I need to go get some help, but first you need to answer a few questions. I'm gonna have to convince some

very headstrong men that you are really here and really a Guardsman." She shook her head.

Piece of cake! Yeah, right, not even on a good day.

"Ask anything you like, Alicia, my dear."

Alicia smiled at his old world style of speaking, ignoring the way her name rolled off his tongue. The lilt of his accent made her think of things she had no business thinking about a man who was trapped and needed her help. Clearing her throat, she asked, "You said your last name was MacLendon? Are you related to Rayne MacLendon?"

"Yes, Rayne is my nephew." He chuckled, but she could feel his sadness. "I am guessing since you mentioned Rayne instead of his father, Alexander, that he no longer lives?"

"No, I'm so sorry. From the stories I've heard he has been gone for some time."

Alicia could feel Drago's sadness and wished there was something she could do or say that would help, but for the first time in her life, she was speechless. The silence seemed to stretch on until she wondered if maybe he'd collapsed. The strain in his voice, as well as the unmistakable weakness she felt him trying to hide, had been evident. Not sure what to do, she whispered, *"Are you okay?"*

Yeah, that was stupid. Of course he's not okay.

"I mean..."

"I know what you mean, mo chroi', *and I appreciate your condolences. I knew it was too much to hope that my brother still lived, but I am glad his son survives."*

Once again Alicia wasn't sure what to say. Deciding to get back to the business at hand, she asked, *"Is there anything I can tell Rayne that will make him believe you are who you say you are and not a figment of my imagination?"*

His laughter was warm but she could feel his struggle as he answered, *"Tell him you know his first taste of whiskey was from his father's flask that Rayne had taken when ol' Alex had a wee bit too much after the battle at Hunter's Cove. Make sure you add that you know he has a scar on his left buttocks from falling down the ladder the next morning after passing out in the hayloft and that I'm the one that covered for him while he nearly threw up his toes during training that afternoon."*

Alicia laughed out loud. It was hilarious to imagine the totally composed, always in control, Rayne MacLendon drunk and falling out of the hayloft, not to mention throwing up in the training pitch. She wondered if Kyndel knew about her mate's childhood exploits. *"I'm not sure I can get away with the comment about his 'buttocks',* she mimicked his accent. *"His mate may take issue with that."*

"His mate?" Pride mixed with loss floated from Drago.

Alicia felt horrible that she'd dropped that bomb on him without thinking. There was going to be so much he had to deal with but that could all wait until she got him out of the hole in the ground. Answering as quickly as she could and pouring all the warmth and happiness she could into her words, Alicia replied, *"Yes, he has been mated for several years and they have a son. They're very happy and I know they're gonna be even happier to meet you."*

Her words were met with a tired sigh, *"So many years..."* She felt an immediate about face in his attitude. *"Well, that is for another time. You need to be going. Get your help and get back here. I have lost too much time."*

Alicia opened her mouth to argue. She wanted to tell him not to order her around, that she had a mind of her own and knew what needed to be done. Instead, she stopped and took a deep breath. It was obvious he was dealing with the little bit she'd told him about his family, as well as what she was sure was pain and fatigue from his prison. She'd seen what just little bits of silver did a dragon shifter, so she could only imagine what he'd been through being trapped in a silver box for a hundred years. He was lucky to be alive.

"You rest, I'm going to get help. I'll be back as soon as I can. Don't worry. We'll get you outta there."

"*I know you will,* mo maite. *I have all the faith in the world in you.*"

His voice sounded distant as she said one more goodbye and took off through the woods. Alicia offered a prayer to the Universe and the Goddess as she ran…

"*Please let me help Drago. Don't let his faith in me be in vain.*"

Chapter Three

Arriving at the house she and her family were sharing while staying with the dragons, Alicia stopped to catch her breath. The entire way through the woods, she'd been going over all she'd learned and thinking about what she was going to tell everyone. She was sure her family would believe her and prayed her sister's mate, Liam, would too, but she was seriously worried about the other dragons. All she could do was try. If they thought she was crazy then she'd just have to figure out another way to free Drago.

Opening the gate at the back of the property, Alicia made her way through the garden and up the steps to the kitchen door. Happy sounds of her mother and sisters chatting about their plans for the day drifted through the weathered wood. She had to smile, they were a crazy crew, but they were hers and she wouldn't trade them for the world. With her hand on the doorknob, she took one last deep breath and slowly let it out.

It's now or never.

Turning the knob, she opened and stepped in. All conversation stopped and everyone looked up. Her mother, Sarah Beth, put her hands on her hips and shook her head. "And just where have you been, little missy?"

Fiona and Brenna, two of the youngest of her six sisters, giggled into their hands and waggled their eyebrows while Sarah Beth continued her inquisition. "And don't tell me you got up early and left the house. I know better, Alicia May. I went to check on you in the middle of the night and your bed hadn't even been touched. So out with it, where have you been?"

Alicia knew she was going to tell her mom the truth, she always did, but it was the fear that Sarah Beth would think she'd lost her ever-loving mind that made her stop and think for an extra minute. And of course, true to form, that extra minute cost her dearly. As she opened her mouth to speak, the unmistakable sound of the front opening sounded, quickly followed by her sister

Hannah's voice. "Hey y'all! Anybody home?" And then her brother-in-law Liam's chuckle. "And is everybody decent? Man in the house."

Alicia's shoulders slumped as she groaned to herself, "Well, hell, now the dragons are here too. Why didn't I just walk in and tell her? I swear to the Goddess, am I ever gonna learn?"

Thankfully, everyone including her mother had walked into the family room to greet Hannah and Liam, so Alicia took her time revamping the speech she had planned to include all the info Drago had given her. One foot over the threshold was all it took before Fiona, the youngest of the sisters in attendance, yelled, "Hey Hannah, ask Alicia where she was all night?"

Spinning around, eyes wide, Hannah gasped, "Alicia May…where were you?"

As if things hadn't already gotten bad enough, the two oldest of their band of merry witches came walking down the stairs. "Do tell, Alicia May," they teased in a singsong tone. "Where were you all night?"

Annalisa, the oldest sister, added, "Better yet, who were you with?" and wiggled her eyebrows for added effect.

Alicia blew out a long breath and plopped onto the couch. "All right y'all, grab a seat. Cause you're never gonna believe this story." She added a nervous chuckle to diffuse some of the tension that had instantly filled the room.

Everyone took a seat. All eyes were focused on her. The room was so quiet her voice almost echoed as she started to speak. "Well, it all started a few weeks ago. I began hearing a man's voice in my dreams." Her sisters all snickered and winked, but Alicia ignored them and powered on. It was a survival technique she'd learned when she was much younger. "He was calling to me. Asking me for help. At first, I thought it was just all the stress of the fight with the *Dorcha,* the crap with Cleland, not to mention Mara being missing in action, but things started to get much more intense. I started walking in my sleep."

The look on Sarah Beth's face said it all—she was worried and more than a little pissed that Alicia had waited so long to tell her. Not willing to stop and deal with her mother's anger, Alicia kept going. "Every time I woke up I was up on the cliffs near the caves. Just recently, I found myself outside the one with the entrance blocked by that huge boulder. You know the one that's almost perfectly round? Anyway, I guess the worst was when the voice started calling out while I was awake. I really thought I was losing my mind, but in my heart, I knew I had to help him. It was like a compulsion but there was no magic. I just *had* to help the man that was calling to me. Yesterday, everything changed. The faraway voice in my head became clearer and for the first time I was able to answer back."

She looked from person to person as they stared at her as if she had three heads, willing them to understand… *to believe*. And just as it had been since they were children, it was Hannah that came to her rescue. "So, you talked to him. What did he say? Who is he? Can you help him?"

Letting go of a breath she hadn't realized she was holding, Alicia smiled at her sister. Being number three and four in a brood the size of the McKennons had made the girls not only sisters, but also friends, and today Alicia needed all the friends she could get. "Yeah, I talked—or thought—to him." She laughed out loud at how crazy she sounded. "He said he was trapped about a hundred years ago by the *Dorcha,* specifically the *Grand Draoi…*"

"Cleland?" everyone almost shouted at the same time.

"No, that's the weird part. He said he didn't know who Cleland was, and after I thought about it for a minute it kinda did make sense, because Cleland isn't that old and we all know how that butthead came into power."

Heads were all nodding in agreement with varying degrees of sadness and anger that Cleland's bid for power had cost their father his life. After a few seconds of silent commiseration, the young witch continued, "And here comes the part that I'm gonna need your help with, Liam."

Her brother-in-law nodded. "Anything you need, Ally."

She smiled at the nickname he'd made up for her since mating her sister. Alicia had never liked anything but her full name but she was kinda warming up to the idea of it, especially when she could see it made Hannah happy.

Nodding, she said, "He said his name is Drago MacLendon...."

"Holy shit!" Liam yelled, cutting off what she was about to say and finishing for her. Awe colored the young Guardsman's words. "You have got to be kidding me? Do you know who he is? Or was?" He rushed on, not waiting for an answer, jumping up and pacing as he talked. "He's Rayne's uncle, but everyone—and I mean *everyone*—thought he was dead. He and his men disappeared like forever ago. Poof! Gone! Never heard from again. And it was a *huge* deal. They were seriously vital to the dragons and their fight against extinction. The man was known as the *Assassin*."

Everyone in the room gasped. Liam stopped pacing and looked around, shaking his head. "No, not the way you're thinking. He was a freaking legend. Still is. He got the name because there wasn't a wizard or hunter alive that could outrun, outwit, or outfight him and his Force. His men were known as The Enforcers and let me tell you, when they set their sights on an enemy, that enemy was as good as dead. I mean I've heard the stories since I was a little *drake*. You've got to go tell Rayne. We've got to figure out how to save him…"

Liam spun around and stared at her for a just a second longer than was comfortable. His brows were furrowed and he bit the inside of his cheek. She knew he was talking to Hannah through their mating bond because her sister was nodding her head even though the room was silent as a tomb.

Oh damn! Bad choice of words.

Alicia opened her mouth to ask what was up when Liam squinted his eyes and asked, "Just how is it that you are the only one that can hear him or speak to him, Ally?"

Oh crap! Oh crap! Oh crap!

The one thing she'd hoped no one would focus on was the one thing her brother-in-law seemed to grab on to. Alicia wished she could disappear in a cloud of smoke but instead, she stood up straight and looked him right in the eye. "I asked the same question, believe me. I mean I questioned him up and down about why me and not one of y'all."

She stopped, hoping that was enough of an explanation and they could get on with how to best approach the Dragon Guard Commander with her bombshell, but no such luck. Hannah stood and walked across the room, stopping right in front of Alicia with a knowing look on her face. "Is he your mate, Ally?" she whispered.

Alicia had no idea what to say or do. But by the way everyone in the room was staring at her, waiting for an answer, she knew she better come up with something quick. So she did the only thing she knew how to do. She told the truth. "That's what he says."

"And what do you say?" Hannah asked, just a bit louder than before.

Throwing up her hands and stepping away from her sister, Alicia walked to the window and stared at the flowers blooming around the porch. She had no idea what to say. It was something she herself hadn't come to terms with and truly wasn't ready to share with her entire family, but now it was out in the open and she had to do something. Her thoughts were in chaos when the low, baritone voice that had started this whole mess asked, *"What do you feel, Alicia?"*

"Have you been listening the whole time?" she demanded.

"No, I was sleeping, and you know we cannot always communicate over long distances. It was your distress and worry that woke me. I had to reach out to you, to make sure you were all right," Drago answered, ignoring her curt tone and pushing confidence at her. She could feel him trying to reassure her and had to admit it was nice. *"So I ask again,* mo chroi', *what do you feel?"*

"You know darn good and well what I feel, Drago, and stop with all the mushy sentiments. It only makes this all the more crazy. I don't even know what you look like. We have bigger fish to fry than discussing our love lives. Now, go back to sleep and I'll let you know when I have everything here sorted out."

"As you wish, mo maite.*"* She could hear the chuckle in his voice and promised to kick him in the shins once he was free and she knew he was okay. Their connection went dead and she turned to face her family.

"Yeah, okay, we have a connection. But I'm not so sure it's the whole mate thing he thinks it is." She saw Liam and Hannah with goofy grins on their faces about to interrupt, so she hurried on. "I know. I know. You two obviously think he's right. Who knows? What I do know is that he's buried in a magical hole in a silver box and we need to get him out. The black magic is too strong for me break through alone. I'm gonna need help and we're gonna need pure brute strength to get that boulder out of the way and dig him out if we find what I think we're gonna find in that cave."

"He's been encased in silver for a hundred years?" Liam asked. "Do you know what silver does to a dragon? He must be one tough son of a bitch." Alicia once again heard awe in her brother-in-law's voice.

She nodded. "That's what I've been trying to tell you. He's in trouble and we need to get him out. Will you help me talk to the Commander? Please?"

"Yep." Liam grabbed Hannah's hand and headed to the door, calling over his shoulder, "Come on Ally, let's get this show on the road."

The walk to the house Rayne and Kyndel had been staying in since they'd gotten back to the Blue Thunder lair was silent. Alicia was deep in thought and figured her sister and brother-in-law were talking in their 'special way' while trying to leave her alone. Hannah had always been pretty good about giving Alicia the space she needed to work through things on her own, and she was grateful for that.

All too soon they came to the back of the MacLendon house. Alicia looked at Hannah and Liam before asking, "How do you think we go about this?"

Before either could answer, the back door opened and Rayne walked out onto the patio. "I suggest you come in here and tell me what the hell is going on. Heavens know Liam is the worst at shielding his thoughts and his little mate's worry is even stronger today." He stood with his arms crossed over his massive chest and spoke with such command that Alicia was walking forward before she realized what was happening.

Looking to her side, she saw Hannah and Liam had identical looks of obedience as they also followed the Commander's orders. When they were about two steps from where the formidable Rayne MacLendon stood, the door behind him swung open and out came his fiery redheaded mate with their son on her hip. She smacked her mate on the shoulder before smiling directly at Alicia. "Don't let Mr. Grumpy Pants order you around like that. Y'all come on in and have some muffins. I just put the coffee on." Then to her husband as she was turning to go back inside she said, "I swear your manners leave a lot to be desired."

Alicia held her breath, not sure what to make of what she was witnessing. Then she saw the look of utter love and devotion in the Commander's eyes as he took his son and leaned down to kiss Kyndel on the cheek, and knew theirs was a match made in the Heavens. It was something straight out the love stories Brenna was always reading and would make what Alicia had to say just a little easier.

Following the MacLendons into the house and taking a seat at the kitchen table next to Liam and Hannah, Alicia prayed for a meteor to hit the house or some other tragedy that would keep her from having to tell her story. Unfortunately, nothing happened, and in no time at all Rayne and Kyndel were sitting across from her asking what was going on.

She told her story the same way she had less than an hour ago, but this time with no interruptions, even though she could feel Liam about to jump out of his skin at her side. "And now I am here to ask if you and the other Guardsmen will help me get Drago out of that Goddess forsaken hole."

Time seemed to stand still as Rayne simply sat and stared at her. Alicia wanted to fidget, thought about getting up and leaving, but just sat completely still and waited. It seemed that was what everyone was doing, including Rayne's usually very animated and opinionated mate, and it was absolutely nerve racking.

Alicia decided to count to a hundred in her head and had reached seventy-eight when the Commander finally spoke. "I understand you believe the man," he said the word like it had quotes around it, "is my uncle, but that simply is not possible. My father and some of the greatest Guardsmen to ever swing a sword moved the Heavens and earth to find Drago and his men and they came up empty-handed. There was no sign of them or magic or anything. They had simply disappeared. There is no way that whoever is speaking to you is Drago MacLendon. I think we should call Kyra and have her see if it is Cleland or one of his lackeys. That is a much more logical explanation. I am sorry you wasted your time."

She'd heard enough. It had been a long couple of hours and an even longer couple of weeks and Alicia was simply fed up. She was going to save the man that needed her help with or without the 'great Rayne MacLendon's assistance, and then she was going to show them all that she was not crazy. But first, she was going to have her say.

"I see where it would be hard for you to accept. Hell, it was hard for me to deal with too. But imagine having someone talking to you when you sleep, willing you to literally get out of bed and traipse through the woods in the middle of the night to find them. Imagine feeling like someone else's life was in your hands but in this case, it was someone you'd never met, never even seen, and they were telling you they'd been trapped for a hundred years and you were their only hope of survival. Can you imagine that, Commander? Can you fathom it?' She didn't wait for his answer.

"Well, I have lived it and I am here to tell you that I will save him and I will prove that he is your uncle because I believe what he's told me. I can feel it here." Alicia laid her fist on her chest right over her heart. "And I know it with all that I am."

She stood up and started to the door then remembered what Drago had told her. Spinning around, she looked up at the six foot five inch Dragon Guard Commander who'd also stood and was apparently following her out the door. "And by the way, the man you are sure is *not* your uncle said to remind you that your first taste of whiskey was from your father's flask after he'd had too much to drink after the battle at Hunter's Cove. He also said to tell you that you have a scar on your left butt cheek from falling down the ladder the next morning after passing out in the hayloft. And I think he said that he covered for you while you were sick during training that afternoon."

Rayne stood motionless with a look of utter shock on his face. Alicia waited exactly two heartbeats before doing an about face and heading toward to door. Only Kyndel's words stopped her progress. "Holy shit! He *does* have a scar on his ass and he told me it was from a sword wound."

Alicia turned again and wondered if it would be easier just to turn in circles until all of this mess was over, but laughed when she saw the blush on Rayne's cheeks and the shit-eating grin on Kyndel's face. The entire room erupted in laughter when the sassy redhead added, "Sword fight *my* ass! No, I guess it's actually *your* ass!" She laughed out loud. "Just wait until I tell the guys this story."

"Kyndel…" Rayne growled.

Swatting his arm, Kyndel laughed even louder. "Don't you growl at me, ya big ol' grumpy dragon. I can tell from the look on your face the story is true." Her laughter had all but stopped. "And it's obvious *no one* else knows that story, so what are you gonna do to help Alicia?"

The Commander looked down at his mate and then at Liam before coming back to Alicia. "We need to call Melanie and Kyra and the rest of my Force, as well as Rory and his men. I'm sorry I doubted you, but you have to understand…"

Holding up her hand, Alicia cut off whatever the Commander was going to say. "It's okay. I understand. Trust me, none of this shit makes sense."

"I do have another question," Rayne paused, turning to Liam and Hannah. "Can you two begin rounding everyone up?" He then added, "Oh, and will your mother and sisters be able to help, as well?" He directed his question to Hannah.

"You know it. They're just waiting for you to say the word."

"Consider it said," was his answer as he turned his attention back to Alicia. Nodding his head for her to follow him, Rayne walked past, opened the door, and held it while motioning for her to walk outside.

Once they were standing on the patio, he asked, "Why is it that Drago can only communicate with you? And you with him? Is there something else I need to know?"

Alicia could see in his eyes that he already knew the answer but needed to hear her say it.

This crap is really getting old.

Shaking her head, she looked out over Kyndel's huge garden and wondered how to answer. Alicia was exhausted, but more than that, she was tired of answering the same question over and over. Not that she should've been surprised. The dragons were very perceptive and highly intuitive, so there was little that got by them. Just this once she was hoping all the other news would trump this one stupid question.

Looking back to Rayne, Alicia gave in and answered the only way she could. "He says we're mates. And before you ask, he's probably right, but can we please just get him out of there and worry about everything else later?"

Smiling the first real smile she could ever remember that wasn't directed at his family or one of his Guardsmen, Rayne nodded. "Whatever you like, Alicia. And thank you for not giving up on me. I know I can be stubborn but it has served me well over the years. Having Drago back is something I never dreamed could happen. I can never thank you enough for giving me back part of the family I lost."

"You are very welcome, Commander, but we don't have him back yet," was all Alicia could squeak out past the lump in her throat.

Thankfully, the back door flew open and out came Liam and Hannah, with Kyndel not far behind. Liam was the first to speak. "We got a hold of everyone and they are all headed to the McKennons'. Hannah called her mom and they're getting ready too."

Rayne nodded and looked at his mate, who'd just started to talk. "Sam is on the way to hang with Jay and me, so ya' know Lance will meet you there, too. Keep in touch. I'm sure the rest of the girls will end up here soon, so let us know if you need anything."

Cutting through the crowd, Rayne approached his mate, scooped her into his arms, and kissed her as if she was the very air he breathed. Alicia knew she should look away but simply couldn't—it was just too amazing to behold. When they broke apart and Rayne retuned Kyndel to her feet, they looked into each other's eyes for just a moment longer. The Commander said something in Gaelic that made Kyndel blush and had Liam clearing his throat, then turned and stepped off the patio before calling over his shoulder, "Come on, it's time to see some witches about saving an assassin."

"Just watch your ass out there, Commander," Kyndel called after them.

Everyone laughed aloud as they followed Rayne out of the yard and through the woods. For the first time since all this had started, Alicia really felt like she might not be as crazy as a bed bug.

Hi ho, hi ho, it's off to save the assassin we go!

Chapter Four

It took almost two hours and four more times through her story to get everyone on the same page and headed out the door to save Drago. For some silly reason, Alicia had thought once Rayne was on board everyone else would be on board too, but boy oh, boy, had she been wrong. They'd all needed to hear her story for themselves. By the time the witches and dragons were marching the path she'd followed so many times it almost seemed surreal. Never in a million years would Alicia have guessed that she wasn't really losing her mind but finding her…well… a man that meant a lot to her.

Nope, can't string those words together. Maybe later, just not yet.

She knew she was being silly. Sooner rather than later, if everything went as planned, Alicia would be face to face with Drago. It was pretty much a foregone conclusion that he would demand she acknowledge their connection, but for right now, she had a little time and dammit, she was going to take it. Lost in thought, she ran right into Rory's—the leader of the Blue Thunder Guardsmen—back. Looking over his shoulder, he grinned. "Not much sleep lately, huh?"

Deciding it was easier to just answer than get mad, Alicia shook her head. "Nope, not much at all."

"Do you have any idea what we're walking into? I mean I know you and your family have some serious magical mojo, so does it feel like anything you've dealt with before?"

"If you're asking if it feels like Cleland and his crew then the answer is no. It's most definitely black magic but nothing I've ever felt before."

"Give the girl a rest, Rory. She's had a rough couple of weeks and has to stay on her toes. This place is damn near glowing with dirty magic. It still amazes me that I haven't felt it before." Kyra shrugged. "Guess my mind's been on Mom. At first I thought she was just out gallivanting but now I'm worried."

"We'll find her *mo chroi'*, you know we will," her mate Royce answered, coming up behind her. "Calysta's a tough old bird. Wherever she is, she knows we're looking. It'll be over soon. I can feel it my bones."

Kyra and Rory laughed in unison but it was Lance, another member of Rayne's Force, who was the first to comment. "And them are some real old bones," he joked in his best good old boy accent. "Heavens know they have the wisdom."

Everyone howled, even Alicia, although every step they got closer to the cave she grew a little more anxious. She and her family had always been around black magic and had fought it at every turn, but Kyra was right, the stuff they were walking into was old, like really old... *ancient*. There was something just not quite right about it, too. Something the young witch had mentioned to both her mother and the incredibly strong daughter of the Grand Priestess, Kyra. Alicia couldn't put her finger on it but it was weird. It made the hair on the back of her neck stand on end.

Creepy shit—and Drago has been immersed in it for a hundred years.

Rayne repeatedly asked about his uncle as they made their way through the woods. Alicia told him everything she could but hated to admit that she'd argued with Drago more than she had assessed his condition. It was one of things worrying her as they started up the mountain to the cliffs. The Assassin had sounded so weak when he'd spoken to her while she was back at the lair. At first, she'd blamed it on distance, but that didn't feel right. She'd called to him to let him know they were headed his way almost twenty minutes ago and had yet to receive a response. Every few minutes, she would say his name or ask if he was there, but their connection remained silent. She knew he still lived because she could *feel* him… everywhere. As soon as the thought crossed her mind, Alicia chastised herself for even thinking something might have happened to him.

He'll be all right. He has to be. He's been in there for a hundred years; a few hours couldn't have made things worse… could they?

Thinking she should ask her mom, Alicia opened her mouth but Melanie, her sister Hannah's oldest friend and also a mate to one of the dragons, cut her off before she could speak. "Whatcha thinking so hard about, doll?"

"Nothing really? Just thinking about what has to be done."

Melanie nodded but the knowing look on her face said she wasn't buying Alicia's nonchalance. Her words confirmed her expression. "I know you're worried. Hell, I would be frantic if it was Jace."

"It's not the same thing," Alicia muttered.

"Okay, yeah, whatever you say. I'll let you have a little more time with your denial, but as soon as Drago is out of his cage, you had better be ready. These dragons don't play when it comes to their mates. And you're boy's been through a hell of an ordeal. He's gonna seriously need you."

Nodding, Alicia murmured, "Yeah, I know. I'll cross that bridge when I get there."

"I'm here if you need me."

Looking up for the first time since Melanie had started to talk, Alicia gave her a smile before saying, "Thanks Mel. Really, thank you."

"Any time, doll. Any time."

They walked along in companionable silence until Kyra and Sarah Beth called out in unison, "Alicia, get up here."

Jogging to the front of the pack, she arrived just as Kyra was removing a copper pot and herbs from her backpack. "What are you doing? We're about a hundred yards from the cave." Alicia knew she was yelling and really didn't care. Her frustration level was through the roof and still climbing. Every minute they wasted was another minute Drago had to suffer, and as far as she was concerned, that was completely unacceptable.

Sarah Beth laid her hand on Alicia's shoulder and spoke as calmly as possible. "Kyra and I both felt a huge surge of black magic right here." She pointed to the spot on the ground where the platinum-haired white witch had placed her copper pot. "Kyra is going to scry for the origin. You're going to need to be patient for just a little bit. If my hunch is right, this is the source of the power keeping your… ummm… Drago imprisoned."

Alicia knew her mother was about to call him her mate. She heard the snickers behind her and thought about telling them all to go to hell. Nodding to her mother, she walked ahead about fifty feet and sat on a rock to think while Kyra and Sarah Beth scryed.

Closing her eyes, Alicia prayed to the Goddess that Drago was okay and that they would get to him on time. She'd never been extremely devout when it came to her spiritual side, but decided if it would help Drago, she would try anything. Several minutes into her prayers, the one voice she'd missed more than she thought possible finally spoke.

"I appreciate your prayers, ceann beag, *but it is you I believe in right now. It is you that will free me from this hell."*

"Sure, whatever you say," she scoffed. "And what did you just call me? I understood the others but I've never heard that one."

Chuckling the low, baritone chuckle that seemed to ignite all Alicia's senses and make it hard for her to focus, Drago simply said, *"Little one. It means little one."*

Alicia wanted to be upset but kind of liked the name. All the same, she felt an obligation to give him just a little crap. "*Little one, huh? Where did that come from? I'm almost five foot ten."*

"It is just how I think of you, as my 'little one'. Someone I can care for. Someone to love. Someone that loves me back. You are my hope and that is something I haven't had in a very long time."

Words escaped Alicia as she sat there absorbing Drago's beautiful words. They touched her as few things ever had. It seemed incomprehensible for her to think of herself as anyone's hope, let alone a Dragon Guardsman's who'd been trapped in a magical spell under the earth for almost a hundred years. It seemed like some kind of mixed up, upside-down fairytale. She felt like the princess who was saving her knight in shining armor. The thought made her giggle, something she hadn't done in a long time.

"I love that sound," Drago whispered into her mind.

"What sound?"

"Your laughter. The only thing better will be when I witness it for myself. I can't…" Drago's words simply cut off and the link between them went dead.

"You can't what?" Alicia asked, trying not to freak out but feeling her blood pressure rising by the second.

Before she could get an answer, Rayne yelled, "Alicia, come here, please." Looking toward the group of people she was proud to call friends and family, the young witch saw black smoke billowing from Kyra's copper pot while her mother, sisters and Melanie stood chanting in a circle.

"What the hell?" Alicia shrieked as she ran to them, still trying to contact Drago.

Squeezing in between Hannah and their second oldest sister, Isabella, she grabbed their hands and chanted along with them…

Under the earth, hidden deep, make yourself known, wake from your sleep. Your power is vast, your reach is long, and your work is finished, time for you to go back where you belong.

She could hear the dragons joining in behind them but needed to focus. Something was happening and she knew with all her heart it was blocking her communication with Drago. Maybe her mother and Kyra had been right. Maybe whatever they were summoning was what was holding the Assassin captive. No matter, the young witch split her attention between contacting Drago and helping the spell.

The longer they chanted, the darker the smoke became and the more horrible the air around them smelled. Alicia would've said it was sulfur, but it held a coppery, almost sickly sweet scent that reminded her more of day old blood than anything else. She prayed it wasn't Drago's blood.

No, it isn't. I would know if something was seriously wrong. He's okay. He has to be okay.

Staring into the smoke, the young witch saw billowy figures forming. At first, they were hard to make out. They looked like the pieces of tissue paper she and her sisters used to turn into ghostly decorations every Halloween. But the longer she watched, the more into focus they became, until she realized they were actual human faces. It all became clear and made Alicia sick to her stomach. They were the people who had been sacrificed by the *Dorcha* to create Drago's prison.

Yelling over the sound of chanting, Alicia screamed. "Kyra, it's blood magic! Look at the smoke! You can see them!"

A collective gasp went up from the witches, accompanied by a low growl from the Guardsmen standing behind them.

"Oh, my Goddess!" Kyra answered into the now haunting silence. "Those bastards locked him away with blood sacrifices and not just any blood, they used witch's blood. There has to be a focus, something that is holding all the magic, and it has to be somewhere below us. That's what Sarah Beth and I felt. The pieces of shit couldn't risk it being close enough to Drago to kill him. It was just meant to hold him… *forever*." Her last word was spoken with such vehemence that Alicia could almost see the white witch shaking with a fury that matched her own. Kyra may have only been five foot nothing, but she was powerful, off the charts powerful… the daughter of the Grand Priestess and the mate of a very strong, very old Guardsman powerful, and she was pissed off.

Putting out the fire in the copper pot with a single command, "*Mhu'chadh*", Kyra looked at Royce standing with his brothers, Rory and Rian, before turning to Rayne then looking back to Alicia. "We have to find whatever they've stored the magic in. It will do us no good to try to get to Drago without it. The magic I feel is crazy powerful and super concentrated. It will keep us from reaching your...*friend* at all costs." Kyra paused and Alicia could feel the white witch's hesitation.

Fatigue battled with worry and added to Alicia's growing fear until just the few heartbeats of silence between her and Kyra almost made Alicia want to scream. Unable to take it anymore, the younger witch growled, "So what do we do? I was talking to him a few minutes ago and our connection just went dead. Now, he's not responding *at all*. I can't even really feel him anymore. I mean I know he's still breathing but other than that, I have no freaking clue what's going on." She was talking so fast by the time she stopped to take a breath, her vision blurred for a split second.

Feeling completely lost, she looked to her mother, "What can we do, Momma? We can't just leave him in there."

"We have no intention of leaving him in there," Rayne answered as he stepped into the circle and walked toward her. "I will save my uncle if it means digging the hole and dragging him out of there myself. I just need you to keep trying to talk to him. Tell him what's going on. He may be able to hear you even if you can't hear him. Drago's one tough son of a bitch. He'll make it out alive. If for no other reason than to see you." The Commander shocked Alicia by winking before he turned and walked to Kyra.

She'd never heard him sound so… *human*. Still thinking about what Rayne had said, Alicia jumped when her mother grabbed her hand and started to speak. "Sorry. Didn't mean to scare you, sweetheart," Sarah Beth chuckled then suddenly becoming serious, she added, "the Commander is right. You have to believe.

Keep talking to him. You're all he has until he can once again see daylight."

"I know, Mom, but it's hard. I'm scared. What if we can't save him? What if *I* can't save him?"

"You just have to believe, Alicia. You just have to believe."

But is that enough?

Chapter Five

Drago had absolutely no idea what had happened. One minute he was talking to his mate and the next... *she was gone*. Not like all the other times when he'd known she was asleep or he'd been too tired to project across the miles to reach her. No, this time was different. He knew Alicia was still breathing but other than that, essentially, she was nowhere to be found. He'd called and called but to no avail. There was just a mass of dead air screaming its ugly silence back at him.

Feeling more trapped than he had in all his hundred years of captivity, the Guardsman and his dragon gave in to their combined feelings of inadequacy and roared. Drago pushed all his anger and frustration into that earth shaking shout of frustration. Feeling helpless was not something the Assassin easily accepted. It was something he fought every day of his captivity but now, without the feel of the woman who had come to mean so much to him in such a short amount of time, he felt lost and completely alone.

Shaking his head the best he could against the silver shackle that anchored his neck to what he feared had become his casket, Drago searched for the calm he'd instilled in all the Guardsmen he'd ever trained. It was imperative he focus. He had to keep calling to Alicia. He had to fight against the flood of pain and agony from almost a hundred years of captivity threatening to drown him. She was his lifeline, and there was no way in heaven or hell he was giving up without a fight. His mate would save him. He would survive. They would be together.

With those exact words forming a mantra in his mind, Drago summoned all his strength and that of the great beast with which he shared his soul and shouted with all his might to his mate. *"Alicia! Alicia,* mo chroí'*, where are you? What is happening?"*

He continued for several long minutes, pausing every so often to listen for the reply he prayed would come, but over and over, his hopes were dashed. Drago was left exhausted and aching without so much as a whisper from Alicia.

"I have to rest. If only for a moment." He spoke out loud for the first time in more years than he could remember. The scratchy, broken echo of his voice was a sad reminder of all the time he'd lost buried in the ground, kept from the ones he'd sworn to protect…kept from the ones he loved.

Drifting in and out of consciousness, Drago continued to call to Alicia through their ever-growing mating bond. He knew it was a weak attempt but he couldn't give up, couldn't give into the temptation to sleep even though it pulled at every fiber of his being. Taking a deep breath, his chest expanded against yet another set of silver chains the *Dorcha* had placed to keep him prisoner, but this time, his constraints felt tighter, almost as if they'd somehow constricted against his torn and broken flesh.

Sure it was his imagination playing tricks, Drago tested the shackles at his wrists and ankles. He shook his head, unable to believe what he felt. It seemed impossible since he'd only ever been able to move a few scant inches, but they too had tightened and restricted his movement even more than they had before. It was at that precise moment he realized every time he swallowed his Adam's apple rubbed against the thick, silver collar around his neck. The smell of burning flesh filled his cell. Not only were his restraints tightening but now they were starting to burn.

Is it not enough that silver eats away at dragon's flesh? Now, it is on fire too? Dear Universe, please let Alicia make it in time.

For the first time since being placed in his prison, the cold, dark tendrils of doubt began to fill the Assassin's mind. He questioned the ability of Alicia and her and family to help him. He questioned the loyalty of his nephew and those his mate had said Rayne commanded to assist in his rescue. It was totally out of character, but for the only time in his life, Drago questioned his sanity and his strength.

Maybe I've finally lost my mind. Maybe this was all a fantasy. Maybe Alicia was all a figment of my very tired, very weak imagination. After all, this is what the bastards wanted. They wanted me suffer. They wanted me to weaken. They wanted me to spend eternity in a hole in the ground without one shred of hope.

Twisting his hands and feet and turning his head to the side in an attempt to relieve even a second of the pressure and pain his bonds were inflicting, the Guardsman felt a slight shift in the earth around his tomb. Holding his breath and his body completely still, Drago prayed to feel the sensation again. Heartbeat after heartbeat he waited to experience even the tiniest movement, if for no other reason than to reassure himself he hadn't gone completely mad.

Deciding his imagination was once again playing tricks, Drago attempted to turn his head in the opposite direction, only to find the shackle around his neck had tightened again, making all movement impossible. One by one, he tested every shackle and chain, only to find the same was true at every point. They had tightened so much he was unable to move at all. It was uncomfortable and frustrating to have lost even the tiny range of motion he'd come to rely on, but what worried him the most was the way the mass of silver around his chest and torso restricted his ability to draw all but a shallow breath.

Drago remembered the words of the *Grand Draoi* as the Assassin drew on his years of training and experience to control his breathing and keep his muscles lax…

"You are no match for the Darkness that will rule the earth. Dragon kin will be destroyed and we will be victorious. Enjoy the rest of your very long life knowing I won."

The Assassin had always believed the evil wizard meant for him to live forever knowing they were still wielding their offending magic over the world he'd committed his life to protecting. Drago knew from Alicia, if she hadn't been part of his growing imagination, that dragon kin was still alive and thriving. It was one of the few things he had to be thankful for, along with the beautiful woman the Universe had created just for him. But maybe the Guardsman had been wrong. Maybe his time was now coming to an end.

Drawing another shallow breath, Drago stopped. There it was again and this time, he knew he wasn't going insane. The earth around his prison had shifted. Unfortunately, almost simultaneously, his constraints once again tightened.

That's it! It has to be what's happening. It's all part of the Draoi's plan. The bastard literally built a failsafe into the spell holding me captive. The wretched beast saw to everything. He knew there was a chance that I could be found, maybe even rescued, so he added a kill switch to the magic. If for any reason I am about to be discovered my shackles simply wring the life out of me. I must admit, I never saw that one coming.

Attempting a sarcastic chuckle at what the Assassin was sure would be one of his last breaths, he wasn't surprised to find it was barely a wheeze. The seconds were ticking by. It was becoming harder and harder to breathe. Drago let his eyelids fall. Not that it made any difference in the complete darkness he'd been subjected to for all those years, but opening his eyes was something he'd become accustomed to since discovering his mate.

Alicia...

Her name floated through his mind, accompanied by the image he'd pulled from her consciousness. The picture he'd held onto every day since learning of her existence. She was simply amazing and he would be forever grateful to her for the few hours of comfort she'd provided after all his years of seclusion. Drago knew it wouldn't be long until he was in the Heavens and knew beyond a shadow of a doubt he would wait forever if it took that long for his beautiful mate to join him.

One more shallow breath, another tightening of his chains, more movement of the earth around him. Silver and heat burnt through his torn flesh. Blood flowed from every wound. His dragon roared over and over in his head at the injustice the Guardsman had to endure.

That roar gave him the strength to send one more message to Alicia, one declaration he wanted her to carry for all time...

"I don't know if you can hear me, but I need for you to know how very much you've come to mean to me. Not just because the Universe said we are destined to be but because of your strength, your intelligence, your beauty, and your heart. You are truly an amazing creature, Alicia McKennon. Know that I go to the Heavens with an abundance of love and admiration for you, my gorgeous mate. Live a long and happy life and know that I will be waiting with open arms for the day you join me. All my love, ceann beag, *all my..."*

And with that, Drago lost consciousness.

Chapter Six

The dragons had been digging for hours while the witches performed a containment spell for the ever-increasing black magic filling the atmosphere. Alicia worked hard to lend her magic while continuing to talk to Drago through what everyone was calling their mating bond. She prayed every second her calls went unanswered that he was hearing her and just unable to respond. It was the most nerve-racking situation she'd ever been in.

"You better hang on, you crazy ol' dragon. You've caused me too many sleepless nights to get out that easily," she joked, wishing she felt as happy as she was trying to make her voice sound.

Looking up, Alicia caught Hannah and Melanie looking at her with a bone deep sadness in their eyes that made the young witch's heart hurt. Hannah gave a weak attempt at a smile while Melanie just gave in and walked toward her.

Moving to Alicia's left, Melanie grabbed her hand and whispered, "I just can't imagine how hard this is on you. I'm here if you need to talk."

Any other time Alicia would've fired back a smartass comment about just trying to be a good person and help another out, but she knew it was useless. It was time to admit to herself, if no one else, that Drago was her mate. It was the only explanation for everything that had happened between them, whether she thought she was ready or not.

Her father always told them that Fate knew what she was doing and with the help of the Goddess, would never give them anything they couldn't handle. Alicia had never really understood that statement until now. It was just a damn shame Fate and the Goddess thought more of the young witch than she thought of herself.

"Dammit, Drago, answer me!" Alicia demanded. *"This is all your fault. You barged into my life and made me care about you and now you're not there when I need you."*

The young witch knew she wasn't being fair but she was tired, frustrated, angry, and most of all, scared. She just needed to hear her Guardsman's voice. Nodding to Melanie, who'd rejoined the chanting, Alicia too mouthed the words that would keep the world safe from the noxious magic attempting to escape their grasp.

Dropping the hands she held on either side of her, Alicia moved to the edge of the cavern the dragons continued to dig in search of whatever the *Dorcha* had used as a focus item when they'd locked Drago away. She squinted into the darkness, listening to the constant sound of metal moving earth as each Guardsman dug with a single-minded focus. They were recovering one of their own. One thought long dead, and they were letting nothing and no one stop them from rescuing the Assassin.

Offering her hundredth prayer of the day to the Goddess and the Universe, Alicia closed her eyes and hoped with all she was. Standing absolutely still, opening herself to whatever heavenly being was feeling especially generous, the young witch let the entities that governed her existence and that of the Guardsman who'd suffered so much see exactly what that one man had come to mean to her. She admitted to them that she needed him to be okay and even more than that, she simply *needed him*.

Drago had slipped under her radar. He had become as important to her as the air she breathed and the people she loved. There was not a world she could imagine where he did not exist and she would do whatever she had to make it so. Summoning her strength, she opened her mind to call to her Guardsman one more time when Rayne yelled from deep beneath her feet. "Kyra! Sarah Beth! Alicia! Get down here! We found something!"

Without a second thought, Alicia dropped to her butt, let her feet dangle over the edge into the hole in the ground, and began scooting on the newly excavated dirt. She heard her mother tell her to be careful and Kyra call out to Rayne that they were on their way but none of that mattered, the dragons had found something and she was going to see if it would help her rescue Drago.

Alicia seemed to slide through the dirt forever before she finally caught sight of the Guardsmen gathered at the bottom of the pit. The darkness was oppressive and she thanked the Heavens when Kyra's flashlight shown from just over the young witch's left shoulder. She also chuckled when the white witch grumbled, "I swear to the Goddess. How many times am I gonna have to tell y'all that witches don't see in the dark the way dragons do? Oh, and by the way, that whole mate sharing thing hasn't happened where my night vision is concerned."

Kyra's complaining seemed to lighten the mood, but her exclamation of 'Oh shit!' when she saw whatever the dragons were gathered around had Alicia standing and pushing her way through the circle of huge men. What she saw was something out of every witch's nightmares.

Sitting not ten feet from where she stood was a four foot by four foot silver box inscribed with every black magic sigil known to witchcraft. There wasn't a single square inch free of the deep, inky markings. Taking two careful steps forward, Alicia gasped and looked to her mother. "That's blood. They carved into the silver and then filled the carvings with blood."

Her mother shook her head but it was Kyra who answered. "More witch's blood. More dirty blood magic." She paused and bit her bottom lip, a look of total concentration coloring her violet eyes.

Alicia counted to ten before the tiny witch spoke again. "But this is where the focus lies. It's in that damn box. Now, we just have to figure out how to get it out of there."

"If we finish digging it out can we carry it to the surface without letting anymore magic loose than we already have?" Royce asked, apparently voicing what the other Guardsmen were thinking since they nodded and awaited Kyra's answer.

"Yeah, I'm pretty sure we've gotten through the worst of the magic that was shielding the box from detection. It had to have been disrupted when y'all kicked the *Dorcha's* ass and saved Melanie." She grinned a wicked little grin before continuing. "Or else we wouldn't have felt it and I'm pretty sure Drago wouldn't have been able to talk to Alicia." Kyra winked at the younger witch before turning to Royce and Rayne. "All right, you boys get this box out of the dirt and up to the top. I'm gonna take Sarah Beth and Alicia with me so we can get everyone prepped and ready to help us open this damn thing."

Standing on her tiptoes, Kyra crooked her index finger in a *come here* motion to her mate, giggling when he bent down and then swooning when he kissed her until she was breathless. Alicia was happy for them, but also felt a pang of jealousy that she had yet to lay eyes on Drago. Shaking her head, the young witch turned and headed back up the mountain of soil, this time on her knees instead of her butt. She pushed all thoughts of anything but Drago's survival from her mind. They were making progress.

Finding the focus was a good thing even if it was the most evil magic she'd been close to in her entire life. It put them one step closer to freeing her Guardsman.

It took almost an hour of additional digging and then careful maneuvering to get the silver box out of the hole and resting safely on the copper rack Kyra and Sarah Beth had constructed. Alicia, her sisters, and Melanie gathered the list of roots and flowers Kyra had given them and made enough sachets for every witch to hold while they recited the spell that would protect not only everyone in their group, but also the inhabitants of the surrounding area from the black magic held within the focus object.

It took forever before Alicia saw the tops of the Guardsmen's heads as they moved to the edge of the cavern. The dragons that actually touched the silver box wore thick, magically enhanced leather gloves, while the others formed a loose circle around their brethren, ready to take over should their assistance be needed. She held her breath as they stepped out of the hole, one united Force, both the dragons of the Golden Fire Clan and the dragons of the Blue Thunder Clan, shoulder-to-shoulder, working toward a common cause.

Carefully moving onto solid ground, the dragons made their way to the copper rack, placed the silver box upon the crisscrossed bars, and stepped back. Kyra motioned for the witches to follow her while she poured salt in a circle about ten feet around the silver box. Each witch stopped at their appointed place, waiting for the circle to be complete and the spell to begin. Once done, Kyra took her place between Sarah Beth and Alicia. The tiny witch looked into the face of every witch gathered and smiled. Alicia could feel her infusing the others with her faith and confidence in the ritual they were about to perform.

When Kyra spoke, it was with an authority that seemed impossible from the five-foot platinum haired woman with the kind violet eyes and heart of gold. *"We gather here today to invoke the help of the Goddess and the Universe we hold dear in neutralizing the dark magic set in motion nearly a hundred years ago by those who would see our world destroyed. We seek to release the one held captive and diffuse the evil enchantment back to the hell it came from. Guide our actions, uplift our hearts, and fill our souls with the sense of purpose only you can provide. Blessed be. Blessed be."*

The witches all followed suit, echoing Kyra's words until they were a chorus of many voices sounding as one, seeking to help the man that was quickly owning Alicia… heart and soul. She chanted with her sister witches until the words came automatically, while watching Kyra and her mother cautiously cover the silver box with a blanket of copper mesh that would hold the focus object and its deadly magic in place after the lid was removed.

Alicia also saw a copper box sitting on the ground beside Kyra. She knew the tiny witch and Sarah Beth were planning to move whatever was in the silver box into the copper one. They were hoping to neutralize the deadly magic contained within, which would allow them to locate Drago.

Holding her breath while watching Kyra and her mother perform the deadly task, Alicia let the chant play over and over in her mind at the same time she called to her Guardsman. *"Drago, if you can hear me, please know that we're trying to get to you. I have everyone doing everything possible to find you and get you free. Hold on. It's almost over. I promise."*

She whispered the last words, hoping with all her heart that she would see his face before the sun set on another day. Letting go of the breath she was holding, Alicia opened her mouth to recite the spell aloud when several things happened all at once, tilting her world on its axis.

First of all, Kyra and Sarah Beth lifted a strange, glowing stone from the silver box into the copper mesh just as Rory yelled from the bottom of the hole in the ground where he and Kellan had stayed to continue digging to make sure no other surprises jumped out and bit them in their collective asses. "Somebody who knows something about magic better get their ass down here right freaking now. We found a tunnel and it's covered with more of those crazy ass hieroglyphics y'all called sigils. It stinks to the Heavens of black magic and rancid blood and…"

His words were cut off as Alicia finally heard Drago's voice in her head. She smiled then immediately started to shake her head as she listened to his words. *"Live a long a happy life and know that I will be waiting with open arms for the day you join me. All my love,* ceann beag, *all my…"*

"No! No! No! Don't you freaking dare!" Alicia yelled in her mind and out loud simultaneously. "Don't you dare give up! We are almost there!"

Tears streaming down her face she raced toward Rayne, screaming as she ran, "Hurry the hell up! We have to find him! I can't even feel him breathing anymore. He's just gone! Son of bitch, Rayne, do *something*! Drago is dying!"

Chapter Seven

Time seemed to stand still. Alicia could see Rayne's mouth moving but heard only deathly silence coming from the bond she shared with Drago. Hands touched her shoulders and others grabbed her hands, all vying for her attention. Her sisters, friends, the dragons…*everyone* was racing toward where she'd fallen to her knees on the cold, hard ground, unable to bear the weight of what was happening just out of her reach. Nothing and no one mattered as long as the silence continued from the man who held her heart.

Her mind raced. The young witch searched for *anything* that could turn back the hands of time and stop the man she was now willing to admit was her mate from dying. Lost in thought, Alicia yelped as a huge figure loomed over her, blocking all light from the sun, while a pair of large, rough hands slid under her arms and jerked her to her feet. Moving quicker than she could track, the same hands that had unceremoniously lifted her from the ground now spun her around so quickly she swayed to the side before regaining her equilibrium. A massive thumb and forefinger encased her chin, raising her head until she was speared by a pair of the deepest violet eyes she'd ever seen, and they were anything but pleased.

"You have to focus, Alicia. Now is not the time to lose your nerve. Snap out of it. Pull your head out of your ass and think. Follow the link you have with Drago and tell us where he is."

Without thought and more pissed than she'd ever been, Alicia hauled off and slapped Rayne MacLendon, the Commander, the man that scared her shitless just by breathing, right across the face. Once again, time stood still, but this time she felt the electricity of her pure unadulterated rage filling the space between her and the formidable Guardsman. It was as if all the air had been sucked from the atmosphere. Everyone stood still, staring, holding their breath…waiting.

Her hand stung from the contact with Rayne's face. A hand print, *her* hand print, was quickly becoming visible on the Commander's left cheek in glowing red reality. Alicia's nerve was failing and fear was quickly replacing the anger that had only seconds ago had been coursing through her veins. The weight of her impulsive action bore down on her like the boulder she knew was still blocking Drago's prison. Unable to stand the pressure, her head fell forward and she focused on a particularly interesting rock sitting between her feet, praying the Commander had more self-control than she did.

Anxiety pushed her heart to beat fast and loud, so loud that all other sound was only background noise. The young witch thought it might beat out of her chest. A bead of sweat rolled down her spine while her knees began to shake.

Alicia was sure there were rules against striking a Dragon Guard Commander, she just prayed the punishment wasn't hanging at dawn. Goddess knew her people had seen enough of the rope throughout history.

Seconds ticked by as she waited for something...*anything*, to happen. Sure Rayne was plotting her demise, Alicia looked up just as the Commander threw back his head and laughed. Not just a little chuckle to let her know everything was all right. Oh no, it was a booming, roaring, all-encompassing guffaw of a laugh that had everyone standing around them immediately joining in.

Regaining his composure, Rayne looked down at her and asked, "Feel better? Ready to save that pain in the ass uncle of mine?"

Alicia stared at the Commander, letting his words sink in. He wasn't mad...not even a little bit. Actually, if she was reading the situation correctly, which she seemed to be if the looks on everyone else's faces were any indication, she'd done exactly what Rayne wanted her to do.

Needing clarification, the young witch cleared her throat and asked, "You're not mad? I mean, I hit you...in front of everyone."

She whispered the last part mostly because she couldn't believe she was reminding him of her actions.

Grinning, Rayne chuckled, "Not in the slightest. You were freaking out. I needed you to focus on something other than your grief. If hitting me helped then it was worth it, but I will admit you pack a helluva a punch, little one."

"What did you call me?"

"Little one, why?" The Commander threw his hands out between them and feigning fear added, "You're not gonna hit me again are you?" His shoulders bounced at his own joke as Alicia quickly shook her head.

"No, it's just…oh, nothing."

Rayne smiled a knowing smile but quickly schooled his features and dropped his hands before resuming his Commander persona. "Okay, now that you're back with us, I need you to focus. I know you said you can't feel Drago at all anymore but that could be the black magic, or he might be blocking your communication for some reason. But whatever it is, I refuse to believe he's gone. Not when we are so close to returning him to the clan."

Alicia could feel the strength of Rayne's conviction and was once again amazed by his unwavering strength and belief. It was something the young witch was quickly learning was innate within the dragons. Both the men and their beasts were incredible. She let his calm wash over her. If he could believe Drago was still alive then she could too. The young witch thought about telling the Commander the words her mate had spoken into her mind but decided to keep them to herself. Rayne was probably right. Drago was just sparing her undo worry.

Yeah, well that's discussion number one hundred we will be having titled, Do Not Scare the Shit Our of Your Mate.

Opening her mouth to speak, her words were cut off before they began as Kyra yelled, "Y'all need to get your asses down here...NOW!"

Looking around, Alicia couldn't find the tiny, powerful witch and then realized in that moment that her mom was missing too. Hannah appeared at her side, grabbed her hand, and pulled her to the crater they'd excavated the focus object from. "Kyra and Mom went down to see what Rory and Kellan found while you were accosting the Commander."

Her sister laughed aloud as they sat on the side of the gaping hole and began scooting over the dirt toward the bottom of the cavern. This trip into what Alicia was beginning to think of as their very own abyss was the polar opposite of her first. There were huge LED lights on poles, like the ones she'd seen when the dragons had remodeled some of the homes at the lair. They lit the entire basin of the crater, making it easy for the young witch to see the tunnel Rory had told them about, as well as her mother and Kyra inspecting the sigils covering the dirt walls.

The Commander of the Blue Dragons had been right. The sigils on the walls matched the ones on the silver box that housed the focus stone, and just like the others, these too were coated in blood. From the look on both Kyra and Sarah Beth's faces, it was once again witch's blood. Alicia shook her head and offered a silent prayer for all the magical people who'd given their lives for nothing more than a crazy wizard's bid for world domination. Seemed to be a common thread with the leaders of the *Dorcha*.

Damn, I'm glad to be out of that mess.

Kyra talked as she continued to examine the sigils and make notes on the little notebook in her hand. "These are all containment sigils. We should be able to remove them with a Banishing Spell, but there are so many we'll need to do it as a group and in sections."

Turning toward the crowd that was gathering, she continued, "I'd suggest candles instead of the lights. I have no clue how far this tunnel goes and I'm thinking your extension cords aren't gonna be long enough."

Royce moved through the crowd and stood next to his mate. Looking down, he grumbled, "I'm standing by your side. This shit's giving me the creeps. At the first sign of danger, you're outta here."

Patting his arm as if she was talking to a child, Kyra nodded. "Whatever you say, big guy."

Alicia grinned but immediately began calling Drago again. It had only been a few minutes since she'd heard what she thought to be his last words but so much had happened that it seemed like forever. *"I don't know if you can hear me but I'm talking anyway. You better know there's no way I'm giving up on you. You just need to hang on, we're on the way. You're gonna be free soon. Siobhan will patch you up and you'll have time to rest and recover. You'll get to see Rayne and meet his mate and son. Then I promise I'm gonna kick your ass for making me worry!"*

She knew she was being tough on him but it was only because she cared… *a lot*. Alicia was using the knowledge Rayne had given her just a few minutes ago… sometimes, tough love was the only way to get through the bullshit life threw at you. There would be time for all the other stuff later. Right now, it was going take intense determination and a whole lot of good old-fashioned luck to get to her mate out of the prison he'd endured for so very long—and Alicia was going to make it happen.

Looking behind her, she found all her sisters and Melanie waiting to begin. Turning back to Kyra, she saw the tiny witch looking right at her. "It's your call, Alicia. He's your mate." Kyra's word hit home.

Alicia didn't even flinch. One nod of the head and she said, "Let's do this. Let's find my Assassin and bring him home." No, she hadn't totally admitted Drago was her mate, but Alicia had given in as much as she was prepared to and that was all they were going to get until they rescued her Guardsman.

Sarah Beth motioned Alicia and her sisters to the front of the pack, handing each of them a white candle as Kyra prepared the spell. Alicia could hear several of the Guardsmen climbing to the surface to grab more candles and the few flashlights she'd heard one of them say were packed in their duffle bags.

Kyra stood, smiling at each witch before explaining, "We're gonna perform the basic Banishing Spell. These sigils are strong but nothing we can't handle. It's only gonna be hard because of the sheer number of them. These little son of a bitches are everywhere." She chuckled and shook her head. "I really hate black magic." Sighing, she went on. "Oh, well, all we can do is get rid of this shit one piece at a time. Light those candles and let's get busy."

In less than five minutes, with candles shining brightly, Kyra lead them in the spell that would remove the power from the bloody writing coating the tunnel walls.

"In the name of the Goddess, the Universe, and the powerful Lord, I banish the fruit of evil cast about this place so many years ago. I place a spell of power and purity on everything living or dead, whether constrained by chains, or hidden in darkness, or

murdered for ill gains. I remove the death, fear and dread. I bring life, light, and love. May no darkness disturb the servants of the Goddess, the Universe, and the powerful Lord. So mote it be. Blessed be. Blessed be."

Each witch echoed Kyra's words as they slowly moved as one unit, drenching the abomination the black mysticism had created with pure white light and magic. It was as if a weight was being lifted from around them as the sigils flashed a bright white light before turning from the deep black of rancid blood to the soft gray of a purified talisman. Alicia could feel the black magic being dispersed back into Hell from where it had been originally called. The souls of those who unwillingly gave their lives so that the previous *Grand Draoi* might attempt to destroy the world lent their power to the spell as they were released into the ether to find their place in the Heavens.

Alicia knew what they were doing was necessary, there was no way around it, but every minute it took, combined with every minute that Alicia wasn't able to contact Drago and couldn't at least feel that he still lived, was torture. There were several times she thought about running ahead and screaming the spell at the top of her lungs but knew that it would be pointless and a huge waste of time, so the young witch did the best she could to control her anxiety and continued to speak the spell. It was then that Kyra stopped chanting and threw her hands in the air yelling, "Stop! Everybody stop!"

Alicia looked around the tiny witch and her mother, immediately identifying the cause of the panic in Kyra's voice. Standing twenty feet in front of them was a wall of intricately stacked rocks completely covered with the bloody sigils they'd been battling for the last hour. Not only was it a deterrent, but the sheer power of the black magic flowing from the wall was daunting.

Taking a deep breath, Alicia asked, "So what do we do now?"

Speaking over her shoulder but still not moving, Kyra answered in a tone that sounded like a whole lot of uncertainty mixed with a healthy dose of anger. "We move these damn rocks."

"But..." Whatever Alicia was about to say was cut off as a force unlike any other she'd ever felt pulled at her very soul. It wrapped around her heart and infused itself in every fiber of her being. The young witch gasped for air. Her vision blurred. She reached for her sister but it was too late. Alicia was falling as her world was quickly turning to black.

Chapter Eight

Alicia woke with a start and attempted to sit, only to be held in place by a pair of huge, unforgiving hands. Looking up, she saw the soft grey eyes of Devon, one of the Guardsman of Rayne's Force. He grinned. "Just lay still. You freaked them all out, Ally. They called for Mom when you wouldn't wake up. I had to play chauffer." He chuckled. "I sure hope no one reports a flying white dragon."

Smiling up at the calmest Guardsman she'd ever met, Alicia shifted her attention to Devon's mother, Siobhan, dragon kin's most respected Healer. The Elder was examining a rather nasty scratch on the young witch's arm and humming an extremely serene tune. Alicia immediately remembered it as a healing song from her youth. It warmed the young witch from the inside out, making her feel almost euphoric.

The older woman smiled sweetly. "You gave everyone quite a scare, young lady." Turning to the side, she called out, "Sarah Beth, Alicia is awake and seems to be no worse for wear."

Alicia wasn't sure what was happening, but for the moment, she was relaxed and feeling no pain. Sarah Beth knelt across from Siobhan, grabbing her daughter's hand and looking every bit the part of a very worried mother. "Goddess help us, Alicia May, you scared the crap outta me. What happened?"

Shrugging against Devon's hands, the young witch chuckled when he jumped while simultaneously removing his hands from her shoulders and apologizing. "No worries," was her response, then to her mother she answered, "I have no clue. It was like something was pulling all the strength from my body. It didn't hurt, it just felt... *weird*. Then it got hard to breath and I guess I fainted. Which is happening way too much lately for my liking."

"I may have an answer for you," Siobhan interjected. When both Alicia and Sarah Beth were looking at the Elder Healer, she began to explain. "It seems that your mating bond with Drago has grown quite strong. I understand it is not something you are happy about but there is not much I can do about that at this point." Siobhan paused, giving Alicia a very motherly look.

Not wanting the older woman to think ill of her, the younger witch quickly answered, "I'm coming to terms with all of it."

"Very well," was the Elder Healer's only response before continuing, but Alicia could see her answer had pleased the older woman. "When a dragon finds his mate and the bond begins to form, the couple start to share certain innate abilities. Usually this process is seamless and neither even realize it is happening until after the official mating ceremony. There are, of course, exceptions, and you and Drago are one of those rare cases. Because the man is in eminent danger of taking his final leave to the Heavens, his beast has taken over control of their survival. The dragon with whom Drago shares his soul has reached through the mating bond and borrowed, so to speak, some of your essence to keep the man alive.

"Since the beast is so massive and because I believe Drago is in serious danger, the dragon pulled a little too much too quickly. Once he'd realized his mistake he shoved it back into you. That tug and push was more than your body and soul could handle, so it shut down until everything was once again balanced within you."

Alicia thought about what she'd just learned and then asked, "But why now? Drago has been in danger from the first moment he called to me. Shouldn't his dragon have worked his Jedi mind tricks before now?"

"I can answer that for you," Kyra said, joining the growing group crowding around the young witch who still lay on the cold, dirt floor of the crater. "The sigils inscribed on the archway of the tunnel leading to the wall of rocks were infused with a failsafe. It was something the wizard working the spell put in to make sure no one ever rescued Drago, at least not while he was alive. But then that punk ass *Draoi* never counted on *you.*"

The tiny witch pointed at Alicia with a big smile on her face. "You are his mate and therefore, the one person that can keep our boy alive until those big lugs," Kyra pointed over her shoulder, "get the rocks moved and we find where they've got him all chained up. We banished the magic of the sigils, now they're doing the heavy lifting."

It was then Alicia heard the sound of rocks bouncing off one another. Something she'd missed until Kyra mentioned it. Nodding, the younger witch asked, "So what do I need to do and can I *please* sit up? I swear there are ants crawling in my hair."

Her sisters, who had gathered around, chuckled as Devon helped her into a sitting position, stood, and headed over to help with the excavation. It was Siobhan who answered her question. "You simply need to continue to try to make contact with Drago. If you feel any strain at all let me know, but I am sure his dragon is only taking the smallest amount necessary to keep your mate alive. It should not be a strain on your system at all. Nature has a way of taking care of its own. This is just one more confirmation that you are indeed the woman the Universe made for our Assassin."

Alicia could feel everyone waiting for her to argue and part of her still wanted to, but that was just the part that wanted to argue about everything. In her heart of hearts, the young witch knew she and Drago were meant to be and just wanted him out of his prison and in her arms. Nodding in agreement but still not speaking the words, the young witch asked, "Is there something I can help with, something I can do? Waiting is gonna kill me." She knew she was whining but couldn't work up the strength to care.

Kyra grinned. "You just lay there and rest. As soon as the big guys have taken enough of that wall down for us to get through, it's gonna take all of us to locate Drago." With that, the tiny witch returned to where the Dragon Guardsmen were making short work of the one thing standing between Alicia and her Assassin.

For the next half hour, the McKennons, along with Melanie and Siobhan, sat around telling stories and generally trying to keep their minds off what they all knew was coming… more black magic. Alicia laughed and worked hard to pay attention but it was useless; her sole focus was on Drago. She continued talking to him, telling him everything that was going on and promising to kick his butt for all her worry.

While she talked to him and tried to keep up her end of the conversation with everyone else, the young witch had been able to locate her bond with Drago and had even felt the extremely strong presence of what she now knew was her mate's dragon. The sheer power she felt coming from the beast was nothing short of amazing. Alicia promised herself to ask Drago to call him forth as soon as her Guardsman was well enough to do so.

I think I want to meet the dragon as much as the Guardsman. Well, maybe almost as much.

A shout of triumph came from where there'd once been a black-magic-wielding-sigil-covered wall. "We're through!" Rayne called. It was the first time Alicia had seen or heard him since waking up. "What's next?" the Commander immediately asked.

Kyra turned toward where the other witches were sitting, waiting for instructions. "I'm gonna go through with Alicia, Rayne, and Royce. We'll see what's up. Y'all get your candles and lights and be ready. I'll be back to get you as soon as I know what we need to do."

Without waiting for an answer, the tiny witch threw her backpack over her shoulder, turned on her flashlight, and headed through the opening with her mate on her heels. Alicia jumped up, jogged over, and followed the large Guardsman. She could feel the Commander at her back and thanked the Goddess when he clicked on his flashlight so she could see.

They'd traveled less than a hundred yards through the narrow, winding tunnel when Kyra stopped and exclaimed, "What the hell?"

Royce shot in front of her, only to be smacked on the arm as she walked around him scolding, "How the hell am I supposed to see what it is if you're in front of me?"

"Kyra…" The biggest of the dragons growled at his mate, obviously wanting to shield her.

"Whatever, Roy. I have to see it to know what to do with it." Kyra sounded irritated and more than a little put out at her mate's protective nature. It made Alicia smile.

While the couple were arguing, she and Rayne moved up next to them and were now staring at a huge silver box embedded in the rock of a cave no one had known was there. Taking a step closer, Alicia could see it was the shape of a coffin and covered in the same nasty bloody sigils they'd been dealing with all day.

From one heartbeat to the next, recognition flooded the young witch's body and mind. With no thought for her own safety, Alicia ran to within inches of the box. Turning, she screamed, "He's in there! We have to get him out. Drago's in there."

Rayne rushed to her side. "Are you sure?"

"Well, if she's not, I damn sure am," Kyra answered before Alicia could form a coherent thought that didn't involve ripping the lid off the awful silver coffin and pulling her mate to safety.

Nodding, Alicia looked at Rayne. "We have to hurry. He's fading fast. I don't know how I know, I just do. Please," she begged. "Please get him out of there."

It was once again Kyra who answered first. "We'll get him out of there, sweetie, I promise. We just have to do it the right way. The black magic in those sigils has to be banished and I need to make sure there's no more surprises that might end it for all of us." Looking at Royce, she instructed, "Go get the rest of the girls, Roy, and have the Guardsmen come too. We're gonna need all the magic, prayers, and luck we can get."

Without further discussion, Royce took off the way they'd just come while Kyra took a closer look at the box. Rayne stood back, pure fury etched upon his face. After several minutes of pacing, he growled. "Why? To what end did the former *Draoi* do this to my uncle? It is absolutely heinous. Do you know what silver does to a dragon?" He paused, simply staring at the silver coffin as if he wanted to crush it like a beer can.

Alicia knew Rayne was talking more to himself than anyone else, so she listened while taking her time to move as close to the box as Kyra would allow and begin pushing as much of her magic as she could into their mating link while calling out to Drago. She could feel his dragon, but even that was weaker than before and still there was no response from the man. The young witch's patience was growing thin just as her mother, sisters, and Melanie appeared with most of the Guardsmen bringing up the rear.

Sarah Beth made her way to Alicia and Kyra. "What do we need to do?"

The tiny witch was quick to answer. "It's just as I feared. The *Draoi* has death magic worked into the sigils all around the seal holding the box closed. If we try to banish the magic like we did in the tunnel it's liable to collapse in on him or something even more horrible." Kyra shivered. "So I was thinking, we need to make a dousing serum, enough to cover the whole damn thing at one time. That should short circuit whatever the crazy ass wizard cooked up and give us the time we need to free Drago. Sound like a plan?"

Everyone nodded their approval and she added, "Great! I need a couple of you girls to go get the gallon jugs of drinking water we brought. I think there are ten or so of them. While they're doing that, the rest of you go collect as much rue, wild rosemary, juniper, leaves from the copal tree, wild celery root, and wild marigolds as you can find. We're gonna need a bunch to banish all the shit those bad guys threw on this box."

Within seconds only Kyra, Royce, Rayne, Alicia, and Sarah Beth remained. The tiny witch and Alicia's mother modified the Banishing Spell they had used before, while Royce and Rayne got as close as they could to the huge silver coffin holding her mate. Alicia watched as the Guardsmen looked for ways to remove the box from the rock. She knew they had to be talking to each other mind to mind, because every once in a while one would nod or shrug. It was frustrating to say the least. The young witch wanted, no *needed*, to know what they were saying.

Alicia's curiosity got the best of her and she blurted out, "What are you guys doing?"

Turning in unison with looks of utter surprise on their faces, the Guardsmen answered in harmony, "We're formulating plan B." Looking at one another and chuckling then turning back toward Alicia, it was Rayne who continued. "If for some reason magic won't get Drago out, we plan to rip the lid right off that damned box and drag him out."

If anyone else had said those words Alicia would've laughed at their absurdity, but with the two most formidable Guardsmen she'd ever met looking at her with complete confidence, the young witch had no doubt they would do everything within their power to free her Assassin. Unable to speak, she simply smiled and nodded, thankful her sisters started returning with the supplies Kyra had asked for. It wasn't long until they had everything they needed and Sarah Beth began putting together the Dousing Serum.

"Alicia, can you make a salt circle around the box? Go right up to the wall and throw some on top. Close it with your magic. Be sure not to touch the silver *at all*. Those markings are nasty little buggers."

"You got it," the young witch answered, grabbing the bag of salt from Kyra's backpack and walking to her mate's prison.

Once there, she got as close as the evil magic would allow and began laying out the circle. In her mind she continually talked to Drago, reassuring him that he would be free very soon. When the circle was as complete as she could get it, Alicia ran and grabbed four candles from the stack her sisters had left laying where they'd earlier been sitting. She knew the ritual she was about to perform was supposed to have colored candles but prayed the strength of her conviction to free her mate would make up for whatever else she lacked.

Closing her eyes, Alicia tuned into the elements all around her. It only took a few seconds until she could visualize what directions were north, south, east, and west. Walking to the north, she twisted the candle into the soft soil and lit the wick. Standing, she prayed, *Guardians of the North, Element of Earth, I call upon thee to be present during this ritual. Please join me now and bless this circle.*

Moving to the East, she did the same thing with the candle and then prayed, *"Guardians of the East, Element of Air, I call upon thee to be present during this ritual. Please join me now and bless this circle.*

And so it went also to the south where she prayed, *"Guardians of the South, Element of Fire, I call upon thee to be present during this ritual. Please join me now and bless this circle."*

And finally to the west where she prayed, *"Guardians of the West, Element of Water, I call upon thee to be present during this ritual. Please join me now and bless this circle."*

Moving to the middle of the circle she threw back, closed her eyes, and prayed, *"God and Goddess, Guardian Angels, and Spiritual Guides please be present with us during this ritual. Bless this circle and keep us protected. No unwanted entities are welcome here. Only pure, divine beings are invited into this space. The circle is cast. So mote it be. Blessed be. Blessed be."*

She prayed for everyone's safety in her own words one more time before lowering her head and opening her eyes. What she saw brought tears to her eyes. Standing around the circle she'd just conjured were her sisters, her mother, Melanie, and Kyra, all smiling, holding candles, and gallons of Dousing Serum, ready to free her mate from his imprisonment.

Not missing a beat, the tiny witch began speaking the revised Banishment Spell. *"Oh Goddess of our hearts and the Universe who gives us life, we come you to again in need of your help. We seek to neutralize the dark magic holding our brethren and release him back into the loving arms of his family. We seek to send the evil enchantment and any left behind back to the hell it came from. Guide our actions, uplift our hearts, and fill our souls with the sense of purpose only you can provide. So mote it be. Blessed be. Blessed be."*

The witches repeated the incantation verbatim three times before lifting their jugs of Dousing Serum and holding them above their heads. *"Bless our actions. Bless our magic. Bless our souls. Lend us your power. Lend us your spirit. Goddess of all, Universe of our birth, God in the Heavens. So mote it be. Blessed be. Blessed be."* Kyra's voice rang out loud and clear. "Douse the box!"

Every witch emptied her Dousing Serum onto the silver box. Flashes of light and plumes of smoke filled the small chamber as the coffin shaped chest holding Drago MacLendon expanded and contracted as if it was breathing. The flames of the candles Alicia had placed at the four corners shot to the roof of the cave while the ones the dragons were holding were extinguished.

The witches again starting reciting the Banishment Spell, this time throwing salt at the box. The sigils sizzled and flashed once again before disappearing completely. A loud moaning filled the chamber. The earth below their feet shook. Rocks and debris fell from the ceiling as a sound like a clap of lightning immediately followed by a heavy roll of thunder roared through the cave.

From one heartbeat to the next, the cave was filled with absolute silence. The flames of the candles at the four corners returned to normal and the ones in the dragons' hands relit as if on command. The silver box holding Drago prisoner gave a gut wrenching moan and the lid flew open.

Alicia gasped as the man who'd come to mean so much to her came into view. He was barely recognizable as a human being, let alone a Guardsman, but not even that mattered to the woman who was finally seeing her mate. Dropping her jug, the young witch raced to her Assassin. Grabbing the silver chains still holding him hostage, she pulled with all her might while screaming over her shoulder, "Help me! What the hell is wrong with you? Get your butts over here and help me get him free! He's not breathing!"

Chapter Nine

Gut wrenching pain attacked his body from every direction. Searing agony unlike anything he'd ever experienced made Drago believe he'd been sent to the fires of Hell rather than the serenity of the Heavens as he'd always been promised. He opened his mouth to scream just as another wave of torture rolled over his brutally battered body.

It felt as if the flesh was being flayed from every part of his body inch by precious inch. The Guardsman struggled against his bonds. The reality of his situation eluded his consciousness. All he could feel was utter anguish. It was obvious Fate and the Universe had decided him unworthy. He truly was in Hell, still chained within a silver box, meant to languish in the Pit to be tortured and tormented for all eternity.

Seeking any solace he could find, Drago forced a picture of his mate to the forefront of his mind. Just one glimpse of Alicia's beautiful face gave him the tiniest respite from the pain. He prayed that he had not doomed her to the same fate. That just because they were mates his little witch would be able to live a full, happy life and ascend to the Heavens where he was sure she belonged.

The picture of Alicia blinked from existence as bursts of blindingly bright light assaulted his ultra-sensitive eyes from the inside-out. Blood-boiling fire the likes of which Drago hadn't known existed seared the flesh of his throat making breathing impossible, just as the ferocious roar of a dragon cut through the chaos of his agony-riddled mind. He reached for his dragon but found the winged-warrior unresponsive. The fit of anger was not from his own beast, but one akin to the warrior with whom he shared his soul.

Another of my family has been doomed to the pits of Hell?

Unable to use the enhanced senses he'd been blessed with as a dragon shifter to identify the beast still seething beside him,

Drago attempted to turn his head. Surprisingly, his head fell forward, his chin touching his chest at the same time he drew his first deep breath. It tasted of fresh turned soil and cool, damp air, not the dank rotten stench of his own skin being eaten away by his silver bonds.

The shackle has been removed from my neck?

Unwilling to trust his own instincts, the Guardsman simply held still, enjoying the ability to breathe. Drago imagined cool, soft fingers gently touching his cheeks and carefully lifting his head upright. He knew it was all in his imagination but he enjoyed it nonetheless.

Another breath and his senses were overcome with the scent of daffodils and sunshine. Again, Drago reminded himself that it was an illusion, a trick his mind was playing on him in an attempt to ease the agony of the constant barrage of torture his was being made to endure, but it simply didn't matter. He would take whatever tiny piece of the heaven that was his mate that he could and hold it in his heart forever. It was all he would ever have of his Alicia.

All thought was driven from Drago's mind as another wave of agonizing pain tore across his chest. His mouth opened in a wordless scream as the breath was pushed from his lungs. His eyes flew open, immediately blinded by a flash of light the intensity of the sun. Squeezing his eyes shut, the Guardsman searched for air, searched for calm, searched for any small shred of sanity, only to come away empty-handed.

Will this torture never end?

Another dragon's roar echoed through his mind, but it was the heart-breaking sob of a woman that cut through all the other noise, wrapped around his heart, and called to his weary soul. Sure he'd lost his mind, the Guardsman couldn't care. It was better than enduing one more second of misery. Gentle fingers stroked his face. Leaning into the caress, Drago focused on the soft, silky feel of another's touch. Human contact was something he'd missed so much and one of the things he'd most looked forward to after finding Alicia, but he knew he was dying, knew that feeling her touch was not to be.

"Oh my sweet, Alicia..."

"Yes! Yes, Drago I'm here!"

"You're here in Hell with me? No! That cannot be!"

The fingers that had so gently touched his cheek now held his face within their grasp. Soft lips laid upon his broken and bleeding mouth as Alicia pleaded, *"Open your eyes, just a bit. Look at me."*

Sure he was being tortured by the devil himself, Drago tried to move his head, tried to get away from the demon pretending to be his mate. *"Get away from me, demon! Torment me no more!"*

The hands held him tight, the sweet lips remained on his, and again the haunting voice pretending to be his mate pleaded,

"Drago, it's me. Please! Can't you feel my hands on your face? My lips against yours? Search our bond. It's me. It's Alicia."

His heart pounded in his chest as his mind tried to reason with the words he'd heard. Drago wanted to believe, needed to believe more than he needed his next breath, that by some stroke of Fate he'd been delivered from his prison, but the pain still wracking his body battled with his wishes and dreams.

It sounded like Alicia. The feel of her mind against his felt like Alicia. The scent infusing itself into every fiber of his being was most definitely Alicia's, but none of it made sense. His mate would not hurt him. She would not torture him. His little witch would seek to heal him, not harm him. Still, the voice in his head begged.

"Please, Drago. Please open your eyes. See me!" Her pleas became demands that were quickly followed by a voice the Guardsman had thought he'd never hear again.

"Uncle, it's true. We have freed you. Open your eyes and see the woman that has worked so hard to save your life." It was Rayne, Alexander's son, his nephew, confirming what the beautiful voice had been telling him.

"Rayne?"

"Yes, Uncle, it's me."

"But…"

"But nothing, your Alicia brought us to you. She has saved you."

Drago dared to hope, summoned his courage and slowly opened his eyes. Immediately slamming them shut, he yelled to Alicia, *"It burns. The light. I can't take it. My eyes are on fire."*

"Turn off the lights! It hurts his eyes! He can't see! Turn them all off!" Her lips had left his to issue her commands but the sweet softness of her hands against his face remained.

Can it be true? Have I been saved?

It took several seconds before Alicia spoke directly into his mind. *"Now try. Open your eyes slowly. All the lights have been turned off, even the candles. Look at me, see that you are free."*

Drawing on his years of training and the little combined strength of he and his dragon that remained, Drago slowly opened his eyes until he could just barely make out formless blobs of different colors. Soft, tender lips again touched his, but this time he could feel them smiling.

"It is you, isn't it?"

"Yes! It's me."

Hearing the tears in Alicia's voice, Drago attempted to lift his arms to comfort his mate, only to be held tight by the same silver chains he'd been subjected to for a hundred years. Roaring at the injustice, he screamed, *"Why am I still restrained? What is happening? My mate and my kin would not treat me so!"*

"Drago! Stop! You're going to hurt yourself even more."

"*Hurt myself! It is you that is holding me hostage!*"

"*No! No! I'm not! We're not!*"

Refusing to be drawn even farther into whatever horrible trick the Universe was playing on him, Drago slammed his eyes shut and tried to pull away, but the hands that touched him so lovingly held fast. Voices sounded all around him, some he recognized, and others foreign.

"What do I do? He thinks he's in Hell imagining all of this. How do I make him believe?" the voice that sounded like Alicia implored the others.

"Let me try to talk to him again. Let me make him see reason," the voice that sounded like his nephew demanded.

"I can't even imagine what the poor man is going through," a woman's voice he'd never heard before interjected.

"He is going into shock. Removing the few shackles and chains that you did made it possible for him to breathe but the pain is too much for his mind to deal with. His dragon has done all he can without hurting Alicia, something the beast would never do, and the man's mind is going to break if you can't get through to him," a mature woman's voice that seemed familiar said with authority.

"What do you suggest?" the voice that sounded like Rayne growled.

"I know!" the voice he so wanted to be his mate exclaimed before speaking directly into his mind. *"You told me to tell Rayne about the time he fell out of the hayloft after drinking too much from his father's flask, do you remember? You did that after calling to me. After telling me I was your mate. Do you remember? Please remember."* Her last words were a whispered plea.

"I do. But if you are a demon you could've pulled that from my mind."

"I am not a demon, dammit. Look within yourself. Find our mating bond. The bond you initiated with me, the woman the Universe made for you. See that what I am telling you is the truth. I'm trying to save you dammit, but you're making it even that harder than it has to be."

There it was, the fire and passion he knew was his mate. The bond that lay deep within him connecting his soul to hers flared to life. It was true! He had been saved. His little witch had done as she promised.

"It is you! By the Heavens it is my beautiful Alicia."

Words escaped him as her forehead touched his and soft drops of wetness traveled down his cheeks. *"Are you crying,* mo chroi'?"

"Of course, I'm crying you big oaf. I thought you were dead." She placed three chaste little kisses along his battered lips.

Before he could answer, the older woman spoke again. "I am happy you have come to your senses, Drago, and even more so that we have found you after all these years, but I'm afraid we need Alicia to move. There are many more chains that need to be removed and we have to get you out of that horrible silver coffin."

Although Drago hadn't dared to open his eyes again, just the tone of the older woman's voice let him know she'd shuddered as she spoke the last words. He was just about to ask her name when Rayne spoke. "Uncle, you need to go into your healing sleep before we begin removing the rest of this silver. I am sorry for the pain you will be subjected to but the horrible metal is embedded in your skin. I'm surprised it hasn't eaten away at your bones."

Trying to answer aloud, Drago opened his mouth, but only a wheeze escaped. Closing his mouth and trying to clear his throat, he thanked the Heavens when the wet rim of a cup touched his mouth. His first drop of cool, refreshing water slid across his tongue and slid down his throat, igniting a voracious thirst.

Tipping his head forward, trying to force more of the heavenly drink into his mouth, the older woman instructed, "Only a few drops, Alicia. We do not need anything else to push him toward shock. Just enough to allow him to speak before he goes into his healing sleep."

Drago wanted to yell at the older woman, to tell her to mind her own business, but he was still unable to speak and Alicia had already answered. "Yes, Siobhan. Just a few more drops. He's so very thirsty."

"Siobhan Walsh?" he asked Alicia.

"Yes, why?"

"I fought alongside her mate, Gareth."

"Well, y'all can talk about that later. Right now you need to go to sleep and heal or whatever it is Rayne told you to do. We have to get this silver off you and get you back to the lair where Siobhan can treat your wounds."

"But..."

"But nothing, you stubborn dragon. Just this once, do as I say."

Chuckling to himself, the thought of freedom and his mate in his arms warming his heart, Drago answered, *"Whatever you say,* mo maite, *whatever you say."* Calling forth the calm required to fall into his healing sleep, the Guardsman murmured, *"I love you with all that I am, Alicia May,"* and quietly floated to sleep.

Chapter Ten

Day seven and Drago was still in his healing sleep. Alicia was beginning to refer to it as his *healing coma,* which none of the dragons were thrilled about, but she really didn't care. She needed him to wake up. Needed him to give her some indication that he was still in there and not dead or dying. The young witch knew she was being irrational. After all, she could still feel him. It was just that he wasn't responding and if she had to be honest with herself, he *was* doing exactly what she'd told him to do.

Siobhan had repeatedly explained that everything was okay but Alicia was impatient. It was day after day, hour after hour, minute after minute of watching him lay there, silent, unmoving, the only indication he lived the slow rise and fall of his chest. It was obvious whatever happened during a dragon's healing sleep was most definitely happening with her mate. He looked so much better now than when she'd first seen him. Then Drago had looked like something out of a horror movie.

The poor man had been a mass of oozing and torn flesh. Alicia hadn't been able to find an inch of skin that the silver chains hadn't tried to eat away. He looked like a massive statue of raw hamburger with long, stringy black hair and a beard of matted whiskers, dressed in whatever tatters remained of the clothing he'd been wearing when the wizards had locked him away all those years ago.

Alicia had wanted to cry. She wanted to raise the previous *Draoi* from whatever pit in Hell he'd landed in and kill him all over again. Even better, she wanted the evil wizard to suffer the way her mate had. The young witch knew it was wrong to pray for vengeance but couldn't help herself. In actuality, she'd been hoping for the destruction of the *Dorcha* for most of her life. They'd brought nothing but lies and pain to her family.

The young witch just didn't understand the violence, didn't understand why it continued all these years later. Could not fathom why one *Grand Draoi* had done this to her mate and another had killed her father. She thought about a quote she'd once heard. "The evil that men do lives long after them; the good is oft interred with their bones." Shakespeare had never been her thing but that one quote had stuck and reared its ugly head over and over in her life. Alicia only hoped she would do something good that would live on after her and that the evil the *Dorcha* had been spreading over the earth for more years than she could imagine would go with them to Hell.

Lost in thought, she missed the sound of the door opening and nearly fell off her chair when Rayne asked, "How's he doing today?"

"Oh, crap!" she squeaked.

"I'm sorry, Alicia." The Commander smiled, trying not to laugh. "I thought you heard me."

Righting herself in her chair even though the grin on Rayne's face said he'd seen her almost land on her ass but was being nice and not mentioning it, she quickly answered, looking back at her mate. "The same. No change."

"The Heavens know I know how hard it is to sit and wait for your mate to wake up. Kyndel got hurt when we first met and I went through the same thing. It was the longest week of my life." He placed his hand on her shoulder. "He will wake. Drago is a fighter if nothing else. He survived a hundred years in a silver box just to find you, he won't give up now."

Nodding, not willing to look up and let Rayne see the tears in her eyes, Alicia stared at her mate. She knew the Commander was right. Could see that in just a week what had been horrible gaping wounds were now bright pink scars in the final stages of healing.

She could now even make out the marking that represented his dragon. The tattoo she knew all the Guardsmen had. Drago's was amazing and covered the majority of his chest and his ribs on the right side with its head just over the Assassin's heart. Once again she imagined what it would be like to meet his beast in person.

The young witch had washed and cut Drago's hair then shaved his face after Rayne commented that he'd never so much as seen his uncle with a whisker, let alone a long, full beard. She'd loved every minute of caring for her mate. Just another indication that they were truly meant to be. She shook her head, smiling at the handsome man laying before her. He was still so very thin despite the IVs Siobhan had filling him with fluids and nutrients. But Drago was most definitely the best-looking man she'd ever seen.

He resembled Rayne in many ways but Drago's air of danger, even though he lay motionless on the bed, was as vibrant as she imagined the man to be. From the tiny glimpse she'd gotten of his eyes, Alicia knew they were dark brown, almost black. She wished more than anything for him to open them again so that she might see them outlined by the full black lashes that had grown back in while he healed.

His bone structure was nothing less than regal. Alicia could imagine him sitting upon his horse, commanding his Force, cutting down every wizard and hunter that dared to cross his path. He was the essence of the moniker he'd been given all those years ago, *The Assassin*. Drago's high cheekbones and aristocratic nose, along with his strong jawline, looked as if they'd been carved out of granite, but it was his mouth that constantly drew her attention. His lips were the perfect combination of hard and soft.

She imagined them drawn in a tight line as he shouted orders or stood over his fallen brethren, but could also see from the laugh lines that he wasn't afraid to smile. Alicia longed to see that smile aimed at her. This one man had burst into her brain, demanded her help, insisted she accept him as her mate, and somewhere along the way, made her fall in love with him. Now, the stubborn butthead just needed to wake up so she could stop worrying.

Rayne's voice pulled her from her thoughts. "Kyra found a tunnel behind the silver box Drago was in. She told me she thought something was behind it the day we got him out." The

Commander pointed at his uncle. "But she couldn't get a good read because of the all the black magic and the silver. It took us all digging around the clock for almost five days to get the coffin out of the rock and then dig another hundred feet, but she was right, it's there. Early this morning, Kyra, Royce, Rian, Rory, your mom, and a few of your sisters went down there to see if they could start undoing all the bullshit the *Dorcha* have carved into the walls.

Your mom said she didn't want to bother you with it and I know I'll probably get my ass kicked, but I thought you needed to know. Especially if they find any of my uncle's brethren buried down there. I know it'll be one of the first things he asks about." Pausing and looking at Drago and then chuckling, he continued. "He's a stubborn son of a bitch, Alicia. I hope you're up for the challenge."

Alicia laughed out loud. "Well, as Melanie and Hannah keep reminding me, the Universe does not make mistakes."

They both chuckled but then Alicia asked, "Do you really think any of his men are down there?"

"You're guess is as good as mine. Since they didn't kill him, I'm thinking they probably didn't kill any of them. Killing one Guardsman is not an easy task, but to try to kill seven as powerful as Drago and his Force was definitely more than the *Dorcha* could pull off, hence, locking my uncle away. I was pretty young when he disappeared but I remember my father swearing he knew Drago lived. He said there wasn't anyone in Heaven or Hell that could kill his brother. Guess the old man was right." The Commander smiled a sad smile. "They don't make them like that anymore."

Alicia felt bad for Rayne. She knew what it was like to lose a father. The hole it left in your heart. Since they were going to be family, the young witch decided it was time to stop being intimidated by the Commander. Standing, she made her way to the end of Drago's bed where Rayne stood staring at his uncle and patted his shoulder. "Sure, they do. There's you."

Before the Commander could respond, a low raspy whisper sounded from the bed. "I could still kick your ass, Nephew."

Alicia stood silent, shocked, unable to move for nearly two heartbeats before flying to Drago's bedside. His eyes were closed tightly but he was smiling. "Oh, my Goddess, you're finally awake," she whispered, tears rolling down her face.

"Yes, *mo chroi'*, but I can't see a thing. The light is like daggers in my eyes." Grabbing her hand, he pulled it to his mouth and gently kissed her fingers. "But for what I have in mind, I think I can feel my way."

Chapter Eleven

It had been two weeks since he'd woken up in the home of his long-time friend, Siobhan. They talked for hours about the trouble Gareth - her mate, Alexander - Rayne's father, and Drago had caused as young Guardsmen, while the Healer had continued to nurse his wounds and pump him full of medicine. Drago felt more like his old self every day and was regaining his sight bit by bit, but had to wear sunglasses pretty much all the time.

Alicia never left his side. She even more beautiful than the images he'd pulled from her mind. His body ached to have her under him. His hands itched to explore her captivating body and his mouth watered to taste her lips to his heart's content. It was all he could do not to pull her into bed and ravage her sensual curves every time she leaned in for a chaste kiss.

Sending erotic images through their link and watching the light pink blush creep into her gorgeous peaches and cream complexion had become one of his favorite pastimes. He also enjoyed talking to her through mindspeak about all the things they would do together if he ever got her alone when others were in the room, and she was helpless to do anything but feign annoyance and attempt to hide her embarrassment.

Looking around the room as he sat up and swung his legs over the side of the bed, Drago wondered where his amazing little mate had gotten off to. He chuckled to himself, remembering how many times she'd already argued with him about calling her little. She would roll her expressive blue eyes, put her hands on her hips, and give him some cock and bull story about her being too tall or too curvy. The Guardsman had set her straight right away and would do it as many times as it took for her to believe.

The sound of Alicia's voice shook Drago from his thoughts. "And just what are you sitting there grinning about?"

Smiling at the incredible woman the Universe had made just for him, the Assassin answered, "Just thinking about how lucky I am. And that you are the most amazing woman ever created, head to toe, inside and out. You are breathtaking, Alicia May, and you are all mine."

Pretending to be suspicious, his mate slowly walked toward him as she asked, "What are you up too, Mr. MacLendon?" Stopping just far enough away that he couldn't touch her, Alicia grinned and then added, "It's not that I don't appreciate the compliment, but I have a sneaky suspicion you're fishing for something."

Laughing out loud because he'd truly been caught trying to butter her up, Drago leaned forward, grabbed Alicia's hand, and pulled her onto his lap before she'd even seen him move. Kissing her neck and enjoying the way she sighed at his touch was almost more than he could handle. Both man and dragon wanted to make love to their mate more than they wanted their next breath.

Kissing up her neck, he whispered in her ear, "I want to go home, to what will be *our* home, and I want to make love to you until we know not where one ends and the other begins. I want to sleep with you in my arms. I want to wake up looking into your brilliant blue eyes. But most of all, I want *you*, Alicia May McKennon, to be my mate. I want to spend all of my tomorrows—whether they are here or in the Heavens—with you. For without you, *mo cheann a'lainn,* there will be no tomorrow for me. My heart will no longer beat and my soul will be barren. For you, *mo maite,* have me made whole again."

Needing to see her eyes, Drago turned Alicia on his lap until she straddled his legs. He had commented more than once about how glad he was that women now wore pants and this was just one more reason why. Holding her chin between his thumb and forefinger, the Guardsman lifted his mate's head until he could look her in the eye, thankful the lights had been turned out and the curtains drawn so he could look at her without his dark lenses. Uncertainty, something he'd never been comfortable with, filled him, but almost immediately, Alicia smiled her dazzling smile and said, "They're happy tears, Drago. You just make me so happy."

"Is that a yes?"

"Oh, yes, absolutely yes."

Unable to resist, Drago laid his lips to hers, pouring all the love and devotion he already felt for the incredible creature in his arms into that one kiss. He *needed* her to know how very much she meant to him, not just in word but also in deed. Alicia immediately opened to him, giving back every emotion he gave to her tenfold. His dragon pushed against the confines of his mind, chuffing for the man to finally claim the woman meant to be theirs for all time.

Easing back onto the bed, Drago's libido went into overdrive. The feel of Alicia's soft, full breasts against his chest, her long silken curls cascading over his arms, and the sensual slide of her legs as they tangled with his, was more than he could handle. Rolling them over so that he was cradled within the comfort of her thighs, he deepened their kiss. His hands slid under the soft cotton of her pink T-shirt and had just touched the silk of her bra when the loud clearing of a throat had him looking over his shoulder.

"I was just coming to see if you wanted to get some exercise but it looks like you already are." Rayne was leaning against the doorframe wearing a shit-eating grin and chuckling at his own joke. "Didn't you tell me once to shut the door if I didn't want to be interrupted?"

"You were ten and complaining about arithmetic and me being too loud. This is a little different. We're celebrating. Alicia has officially agreed to be my mate. Now get the hell outta here," Drago growled, returning his attention to Alicia, only find her hands covering her mouth while she tried not to laugh.

"Congratulations to you both." Rayne sounded truly pleased for them as Drago was thinking of how best to relieve Alicia of her clothing.

But the moment was gone. Pretending to be annoyed, she swatted his shoulder and scolded, "Get off me, you beast."

Never one to be out done, Drago covered her mouth with his, kissing her so completely they were both struggling to breathe when he pulled away. "Beast, indeed, *mo chroi'*. Just wait until I get you alone then you shall see what a beast I can be."

Waggling his eyebrows, Drago used his enhanced speed and was standing at the end of the bed giving her a wink before his little witch could wipe the satisfied smile from her face. Looking to his nephew, the Assassin grumbled, "I'll deal with you later."

"How about now? In the training pit? Ten minutes?"

Sitting up, straightening her clothes and chastising at the same time, Alicia argued, "No, no, no. It's too soon. There's no way you're ready to go out there and train with…with…real swords with sharp points and just…no."

Drago bit the insides of his cheeks to keep from smiling. Alicia was simply adorable. The way she cared for him and always had his best interest at heart was the best feeling *ever*. He knew she was worried, but even though his eyesight had not completely returned and he would have to wear his dark lenses, it was time for him to return to the world. His little witch would just have to understand.

Looking to Rayne, he answered. "I'll meet you outside. Give me a minute."

Nodding, the Commander winked at Alicia then turned and left.

Sitting next to his mate on the side of the bed, Drago slid his fingers through hers, lifted her hand to his lips, and spoke directly into her mind while laying butterfly kisses on each of her elegant fingers. *"I will be fine*, mo ghra'. *You can come along if you wish. I simply need to get back out there. I know Kyra, Royce, and his brothers are close to finding the* Dorcha *and I want to be ready when they do."*

Alicia tried to interrupt but even though they were using mindspeak, he placed the tips of the fingers of his free hands on her lips and continued, *"I'm ready to have a sword in my hand again. It's one of the few things that hasn't changed in the hundred years I've been locked away. This is something I have to do. It may not be the same* Draoi *that imprisoned my men and me but it is still the same bloody black magic and I am sworn to remove it from the earth. Please understand. It is all I can do since we still have no clue where my brethren are."*

He watched a myriad of emotions cross Alicia's expressive face and knew the moment she'd relented to his plea. Kissing the tip of her nose, Drago stood and made his way to the closet to get dressed. The Guardsman knew his little witch was sitting on the bed watching his every movement just as she'd done since the moment he'd awakened, so he let the soft cotton pants she'd called sweats slide to the floor and stood with his naked backside showing just a little longer than was necessary.

When he turned, Alicia was shaking her head and grinning from ear to ear. "Thanks for the show." She giggled as she raised what she'd earlier explained was her cell phone and flashed a picture of him.

I still cannot figure out what a phone is much less how something you are supposed to use to talk to others takes photos.

"Alicia May…" Drago growled.

"Drago Magnus…" Alicia growled right back, raising an eyebrow that made the Assassin laugh out loud.

"I see Rayne has been running his mouth again."

"He might have shared a few things with me." His mate batted her eyes and tapped her index finger to her chin.

It took everything in him not to slam and lock the door and make love to his mate the way he'd been dreaming of since first touching her mind. But Alicia was finally onboard with him returning to the training pit and not even the thought of her naked was going to stop him. It wasn't that he was going to let her keep him from going, but having her blessing went a long way to making his training much easier. He knew there would be compromises. Rayne had already prepared him for modern women and Drago was doing his best to respect what his nephew had explained as *Alicia's boundaries*.

He loved her and there was nothing he wouldn't do to keep her happy, even if it meant changing everything he'd ever known. She was his world…*period.*

Chapter Twelve

"That all you got, old man?" Kellan, the scarred Guardsman from the Blue Dragons teased.

"Seems like I have *you* on the run 'young'un'… and I'm half-blind," Drago countered, laughing aloud as he blocked a particularly sharp jab. He loved that the others weren't taking it easy on him. It showed they still respected him, which meant more than the Assassin wanted to admit.

"Yeah, well, even after being locked away for a hundred years you are still the notorious Drago MacLendon. The Assassin that makes hunters run for cover, wizards wet their robes, and ladies drop their panties at your feet, are you not?"

The training pitch roared with laughter but it was the scent of sunshine and daffodils that had Drago spinning on his heels. "Ladies drop their panties at your feet, do they, Mr. MacLendon? I guess I better watch out for the competition," Alicia teased as she leaned against the wooden fence separating the sandy training pitch from the rest of the lair.

Drago's depth perception was still off and his eyesight fuzzy but he'd know his mate anywhere. Returning his broadsword to the sheath at his waist, the Guardsman walked to where Alicia stood.

"There is no other but you, *mo ghra'*. Tell me, what brings a beautiful lady like you to a dirty place like this?" he joked, swallowing her chuckle as he leaned in to give her a kiss.

As Alicia pulled back, Drago could see the dreamy look in her eyes, the look he'd put there, and his pride soared. His mate was perfect. She was all he'd ever need. Needing to kiss her just one more time, the Guardsman moved toward his little witch again. Unfortunately, his intentions were cut short by a smiling redhead carrying a baby that could've have been Rayne when he was a little boy.

"So you're the Assassin they all keep telling me about, huh?" Her southern accent suited her to a tee, perfectly complementing the twinkle in her eye and the sass in her step.

"And you must be the woman that has my nephew wrapped around her little finger." The Guardsmen behind him chuckled and teased Rayne while Drago just winked at his nephew's mate.

"You know it." She winked back. "I'm Kyndel and this little guy is James Alexander MacLendon, Jay for short. Glad to see you up and around."

"Thank you." Looking at the baby, he commented, "He's the spitting image of his father and his grandfather, with the mischief of his mother in those little green eyes." Turning to Rayne, Drago continued, "You did well, kid. Your mother and father would be so proud."

His nephew gave a single nod before the Assassin turned back to Kyndel and Jay just as Rayne's mate teased, "Hey! I helped ya' know."

Once again the training pit was roaring with laughter as Drago looked to his mate for help. Shaking her head, Alicia's only comment was, "You got yourself into this, big man. Now, you gotta get yourself out."

Turning toward Kyndel, he bowed at the waist—even though Rayne and Alicia had told him several times men did not do that anymore—and apologized. When he looked up, her shoulders were jumping with her contained laughter and to his surprise, the baby was reaching out to him. Drago was hardly upright before Kyndel was lifting Jay over the fence.

The Assassin's first instinct was to back away, but one look from Alicia had him holding the baby like an old pro. Drago knew his little witch was sizing him up as a future father and there was no way he wasn't going to do everything in his power to live up to her expectations.

Jay was all hands and a mass of drooling happiness. By the time Rayne took the child from Drago's arms, the Assassin's dark glasses were covered with tiny wet fingerprints and his face had been covered with open mouth baby kisses. Alicia watched the entire scene with a silly grin on her face and a twinkle in her eyes that said he'd exceeded all her hopes.

Making his way the few steps to stand in front of his mate, Drago just smiled, knowing life with Alicia was going to be outstanding. He thought of their children and hoped for little girls with long red curls and bright blue eyes just like their mother's. The only problem he could see was keeping the boys away, because no daughter of his would date until she was at least forty.

His thoughts were cut short when Kyndel asked, "Why don't y'all come to dinner? I was thinking about steak and baked potatoes. Sound good?"

"Sounds delicious," Drago quickly answered then looked to Alicia. "Is that all right with you?"

Nodding, she agreed, "Sounds good to me." Then turning to Kyndel, she added, "You better have a side of beef, he's been a bottomless pit since waking up." Alicia hooked her thumb at him. "He might just eat you out of house and home."

Kyndel laughed. "I come prepared. This isn't my first rodeo. I've been around these big lugs long enough to know there's not a one of them that can't put away their own weight in meat."

Kellan and Declan had joined the group after dismissing the younger Guardsmen who had been training. Declan was the first to speak. "Is that an open invitation?" He smiled his cheesy smile and nodded his head like a little boy.

"You'd think you'd never eaten, boy," Drago kidded.

With the most serious expression the Assassin had ever seen on Declan's face, which was saying something since Drago had known Declan since the younger man was a Guardsman in training, the Blue Dragon answered, "Just wait till you taste Kyndel's cooking. You'll be begging for an invitation with the rest of us next time."

Grinning from ear to ear, Kyndel chuckled. "Sure, y'all come on. Rayne can get the grill started and if Alicia doesn't care she can help me keep up with Jay. You guys are gonna have to wash potatoes and shuck corn."

Declan and Kellan, who were already halfway over the fence, readily agreed while Drago turned to walk to the gate. His depth perception wasn't returning as quickly as he'd hoped and there was no way he was going to take the chance of falling on his face in front of a pitch full of younger men. Assassin or not, a bruised ego just would not do. Alicia met him at the gate, immediately threading her fingers through his as they followed the others to Kyndel and Rayne's.

Walking through the lair, Drago nodded to the people as they passed. Some he remembered and some he knew resembled those he'd fought beside all those years ago. Alicia's hand in his just felt right; things were exactly as they were meant to be. All that was left was to settle the score with the *Dorcha* and then he would be free to mate his little witch. They would have the happily ever after she so richly deserved.

Once they arrived at the house Rayne and Kyndel were staying in, everyone got busy getting dinner ready. He and Alicia sat in the kitchen playing with Jay while Kyndel issued orders to Declan and Kellan. It wasn't long before Rayne hollered for Drago to join him on the patio.

Kissing Alicia on top of the head, he made his way out the door with two beers and the platter of steaks Kyndel had handed him as he passed by. "Here ya go. From your mate." Drago handed Rayne the steaks. "And from me." The Assassin chuckled as he handed his nephew one of the beers.

"Thank you for both." Rayne set the beer on the side of the grill and began placing the steaks on a huge stainless steel monstrosity the likes of which Drago had only heard about. He knew it was a grill from previous conversations but he had to admit to being impressed. His last experience with grilling meat had been with an iron grate over an open fire.

His nephew must've seen his surprised look because he started to explain. "There's propane, a type of fuel, in there." He pointed to a white tank mounted to the bottom of the stainless steel housing. "All I have to do is push this igniter," Rayne pointed to a large red button on the front of the grill, "and a flint is struck and the fire is lit. It takes mere minutes until it's hot enough to cook. It'll go about five hours total before I have to refill the tank."

"Pretty amazing." Drago shook his head. "I've missed so much."

"You're catching up pretty quickly," Rayne answered over his shoulder while placing the meat on the grill.

"Yes, I know it will take time but I'm looking forward to learning. Alicia tells me to slow down, take it easy, rest and recuperate, but it's not in my nature."

"That's the damn truth." Rayne laughed as he turned and took the seat next to his uncle. "You never let any grass grow under your feet."

"Not gonna start now either…"

Drago never got to finish his statement as Rayne stood and looked up. Following suit, the Assassin was thankful the sun was already setting on the other side of the house because he never would've been able to see the three blue dragons descending from the sky even with his dark lenses. It did his heart good to see dragons in flight after so many years, even though he could feel the huge amount of magic they were using to keep from being seen.

No sooner had the dragons touched down than a tiny platinum blonde the Assassin knew to be Royce's mate all but flew off the back of the big man's dragon. He'd met her right after waking from his healing sleep and thanked her profusely for all she'd done to help Alicia and her family free him. The Assassin had been shocked at how much like a fairy she looked and even more surprised by the power contained in her petite frame.

In the next breath, the O'Reilly brothers appeared in place of their beasts. Not wasting a second, Royce called to Rayne and Drago through mindspeak. *"Kyra thinks we've found Cleland's hiding spot."*

"He was at the end of the tunnel?" Rayne asked while Drago stood and moved to stand beside his nephew to watch the approaching Guardsmen and Royce's mate.

"Sure seems that way. Kyra and the McKennons battled some serious demon powered black magic to remove roadblocks the likes of which I haven't seen since the old days. Several of them even took our dragon magic to crack, but after we got through another of those damned stone walls, Kyra felt Calysta's presence. It was just for a second but she said it was strong. So, it's just like we figured—the Dorcha has the Grand Priestess."

Royce paused and Rian, the older of the O'Reilly's and the Head Elder of the Blue Thunder Clan, continued. *"Sarah Beth confirmed what Kyra felt and also said she would know Cleland's stench anywhere, so I'm positive we've got the bastards."*

"Yeah, we've got 'em, but we have about another five feet to dig out and if I'm not mistaken, which I rarely am, another stone wall to get through," Rory, the youngest of the O'Reilly's, added.

Alicia joined Drago and Rayne on the patio and he'd just barely had a chance to get her up to speed with what was happening before Royce, his mate, and his brothers arrived. Kyra looked like she was ready to spit nails and her comments confirmed the Assassin's thoughts. "I swear to the Goddess I will turn that stupid son of a bitch into a toad and keep him in my kitchen window for the next hundred years if one hair on my mom's head is harmed."

Drago could feel Kyra's power building and knew it was just a matter of time before the very powerful witch unleashed her wrath on the very deserving *Grand Draoi*. He wanted to be there when it happened. The Assassin wanted to be part of the fight... *needed* to be part of the fight. It was the final step to putting the last hundred years behind him and getting on with his new life with his gorgeous mate.

Nothing would stand between him and beating the life out of every *Dorcha* wizard he could get his hands on. His eyes may not be what they used to be but his other senses were razor sharp and he would not be denied. Drago could feel Alicia's eyes on him, could feel and hear what she was thinking. His mate knew what he was planning. She didn't approve or agree, but she supported him and that meant the world.

"Do what you have to do but do not *get hurt. I swear by the Goddess and the Universe I will nurse you back to health just to kick your ass."*

He looked into her eyes, letting her see the honesty as he spoke, *"I would never do anything that would keep me from spending the rest of my life loving you,* mo maite. *I will slay the Dorcha and return to you. That is simply how it will be."*

The Assassin hadn't realized he wasn't shielding until Alicia's eyes grew large as she looked over his shoulder. Turning around, Drago saw his nephew, Kyndel, the O'Reilly brothers, Kyra, and Declan and Kellan, who had also joined them, all watching him and his mate. Their looks said they'd heard every word and the single nod of solidarity they all gave him said they'd fight by his side.

"Well, what are we standing here for? Let's eat this food and plan the fight. I need to get this over with so I can officially mate this beautiful woman."

Grabbing Alicia around the waist, Drago lifted her off the ground and kissed her soundly.

Sealed with a kiss. Watch out, assholes, here we come.

Chapter Thirteen

Alicia was relieved when her mom, her sisters, Melanie, Jace, and Liam showed up. She'd began to wonder if they were still in the tunnel and was about to go find them. There hadn't been a lot of time to connect with her family during Drago's convalescence and she really missed them. Especially after hearing from Kyra, all they'd had to do to get through the spelled tunnel.

Everyone was talking at once, explaining what had been happening while Alicia was otherwise engaged. She tried to listen to all the different conversations going on around her but lost focus when she noticed Drago sitting to the side, all alone, deep in thought. Extracting herself from her family, the young witch made her way to her Guardsman.

"Whatcha thinking about?" she asked, knowing what was on his mind but needing to hear him say it.

"Just appreciating how different my life is now than it was a hundred years ago. Thinking about how, back then, I would have run off without a second thought, with no regard to my own welfare and battled the *Dorcha* to the death if that is what it took."

He finally looked at her and the love she saw in his eyes was staggering. When he reached up, took her hand in his, and pulled her onto his lap, she went willingly. Alicia instinctively cuddled into his chest without a thought about her friends and family seeing their public display of affection. For the first time in her life, the young witch knew where she belonged and was going to hold on to her future with both hands.

Drago wrapped his arm around her waist before he laid his cheek on the top of her head and again started to speak. "Now, I have you. I have something to come home to. I even have the family I was sure would be dead and gone if I ever got out of that hole in the ground. It is an understatement to say my perspective has changed, but it has. So I was just sitting here thinking that I want to make sure we rid the world of the *Dorcha* once and for all."

Sitting up so she could look her mate in the eyes, Alicia lifted his dark glasses to the top of his head. She was thankful the sun had gone down and they were in the darkest corner of the house so she could see the deep, dark brown of his eyes. Alicia put her free hand on his cheek and smiled. "Go do what you do best. Take down the bad guys. Make the world safe for the rest of us. Watch your back and remember... I love you."

His smile was brighter than she'd ever seen and when Drago kissed her, something inside her clicked into place. It was as if the final piece of the puzzle that was her life had been found. Alicia had heard Melanie and Hannah talking about what it felt when they truly accepted their mates, but nothing could've prepared her for what she was feeling in that very moment in the embrace of the man she was destined to spend the rest of her life with.

Their kiss went on and on. Alicia wished she and Drago were alone and was just about to suggest it when a round of applause and cat calls sounded behind them. Moving back just far enough to look into Drago's squinted eyes, she chuckled, "Guess we better behave."

Leaning his forehead against hers, he answered. "Only for now, *mo chroi'*, only for now."

She put his glasses back over his eyes, winked, and jumped off his lap. Turning to everyone else, Alicia pretended to be annoyed, "Show's over people. Let's get ready to kick some wizard butt, okay?"

"Yeah, yeah, yeah…" her brother-in-law, Liam, teased before ducking just in time to miss the throw pillow Alicia aimed at his head.

"Alicia is right. We need to get everything decided and get back down to that tunnel before Cleland knows we've found him," Rian commented.

The Leader of the Blue Dragons seemed unusually agitated even considering the fight they were facing, but Alicia decided not to worry about it. She had no doubt he had a hundred times more concerns than she could imagine, being the Head Elder of the Blue Thunder Clan at such a young age.

Drago stood next to her and asked, "So what's the plan?"

"You're not leading the charge?" Rayne questioned with half a grin on his face.

"No, I'm going to follow on this mission, but you can be sure I'll cut down every wizard who dares breathe in my direction."

Rayne nodded, as did all the Guardsmen, followed by every member of her family. Drago had given the call to action. The dragons and the witches were going into battle together to exterminate their common enemy. Alicia was nervous, excited, apprehensive, and more than ready to put an end to the ones that had taken so much from her.

"Are you staying here with Kyndel or going to your mother's?" Drago asked.

"I'm going with y'all."

Her mate turned, brow furrowed, his lips thin with a frown of disapproval, and shook his head. "No, you most certainly are not."

Taking a step back, Alicia put her hands on her hips and started to argue. "What do you mean 'I most certainly am not'? Of course I am. In case it has escaped your notice, I'm a witch, just like her and her and her." She pointed to three of her sisters as she got madder by the second. "If they go, I go, and from what I heard it's gonna take all the magic we've got to sneak up on Cleland, take out all the *Dorcha* in the place, and save Calysta. Not to mention, I'm hoping like hell we find my little sister, Mara, while we're at it. Did you forget about her? Did you forget that I told you she's been missing as long as the Grand Priestess? Well, I didn't. I didn't stand in your way when you said it was something you had to do. What right do you have to keep me from going?"

Alicia knew she was yelling by the time she paused to take a breath, but she was too pissed to care. She had absolutely no idea how she could love a man as much as she loved Drago and be so incredibly mad at him at the same time. Thoughts of kicking his ass and kissing him silly tumbled over one another in her mind, adding fuel to her anger until she was sure steam was rolling out her ears.

Her friends and family had become suspiciously quiet and her mate was just standing staring at her as if he wasn't sure how to respond. All of that combined made Alicia even madder. Gearing up to start railing at Drago again, she lost all focus when her mate nodded and calmly said, "You're right. I had no right to tell you what to do. You are a grown woman whose opinion and judgement I respect. All I will say is that should you get hurt, I will nurse you back to health just so I can spank your precious bottom every day of our very long lives together."

Drago's words took all the fight out of the young witch. Shaking her head, she chuckled, "And you had to use my own words, or your version of them, against me didn't you?"

"Would you have it any other way?" The Assassin didn't wait for her response before swooping in and kissing her until she couldn't remember what they were fighting about.

Pulling back but turning her around and tucking her close to his side and then wrapping his arm around her shoulders, Drago asked, "Are we all ready now?"

"We've been ready, old man, just waiting on you," Rory teased as he headed out the door.

"We will see who is the old man," was Drago's response as Alicia grabbed her knapsack and took his hand.

Here we go. Goddess protect us all.

Chapter Fourteen

"What are you doing, *ceann beag*?" Drago asked as Alicia sat down on the side of the crater leading to the tunnel where he'd been kept.

"I'm gonna slide down this hill on this burlap bag like I always do, why?"

"You most certainly are not," he growled, scooping up his mate, laying her over his shoulder, and jumping to the cavern floor. Setting her feet on the ground, he grinned. "There *are* advantages to having a dragon as a mate."

Attempting to tame her curls, Alicia huffed a few stray hairs out of her face and glared at him. "Yeah, but a little warning *before* the caveman routine would be nice."

"So not gonna happen, Ally," Melanie laughed as she walked by. "These guys thrive on caveman."

"Hey! Not fair, *mo ghra'*, not fair at all," Jace protested with a grin on his face.

"Whatever," Melanie rolled her eyes.

Drago had to smile at the comradery they all shared. It was something he had sorely missed and was thrilled to have back. Looking around, he saw his nephew striding toward them with a look of command on his face.

"All right, time to get moving. I'm ready to put these bastards in the ground. What about you?" Rayne's question was more of a command but it didn't stop everyone from wholeheartedly agreeing.

Positioning Alicia behind Royce and in front of himself, Drago prayed she would be protected from whatever they were walking into. It wasn't that he didn't respect her power; the Heavens knew he could feel its magnitude coursing through every fiber of her being.

Alicia's magic was amazing but she was his mate. His to protect. Knowingly letting her walk into danger went against everything the man *and* the beast believed in. His dragon chuffed in his head to let the Guardsman know he was most definitely not thrilled with their mate being anywhere near the black magic they had already sensed. Drago agreed but explained it was what they had to do.

All too quickly, the group arrived in the exact spot the Assassin had spent the last hundred years of his life. Lying to the side were the remnants of the silver coffin he'd been imprisoned in. Bit and pieces of broken chains and shackles littered the floor, haunting reminders of what he'd endured. Drago recalled Alicia telling him how Rayne had lost control when he saw his uncle, partially calling forth his dragon and ripping the silver collar from Drago's neck and the chains from his chest.

The nightmare was over but the pain would live on. Drago knew killing Cleland and his minions wouldn't give him back the years he'd lost, nothing could do that, but it would stop them from hurting anyone else. No, the reigning *Draoi* wasn't the wizard that had locked the Assassin away but from what Drago had been told, Cleland was just as menacing, just as detrimental to anyone that opposed him, and that meant destroying him and all he stood for.

Alicia looked over her shoulder and reached to him. *"You okay?"*

Taking her hand, he smiled. *"I am fine,* mo ghra'. *That is the past."* He glanced one last time at the broken coffin. *"You are my future."*

Drago felt the love Alicia was pouring through their bond and for the hundredth time since waking thanked the Universe for the gift of his mate. The group continued through the hole in the cavern wall the dragons had created. The air was oppressive. Although the black magic from the sigils had been banished, there was still the unmistakable stench of sulfur and brimstone. Demon magic was heinous. It left not only a mark on the soul of the user but a scar on the earth itself. It was an abomination against nature, against life itself, and brought only death. That Kyra and the McKennons had dealt with such an enormous amount of the offending magic was amazing. Drago hadn't thought it was possible but he respected them even more than he had before.

Approaching the archway, the Assassin could see the excavation left to be done and grabbed a pickax. Starting toward the wall with the other Guardsmen, he watched Alicia make her way to where her family and Kyra were preparing more sachets. Drago couldn't help feeling like his mate shouldn't be anywhere near the *Dorcha*, demons, or black magic no matter how powerful she was, or that she had her own score to settle with the evil wizards and their leader. Shaking his head, he prayed for the safety of everyone present—but especially—his mate.

In less than an hour, Drago, Rory, and Rian had broken though the rock wall. Their sheer size dictated that only three of them could fit shoulder to shoulder in the tunnel and even at that, they'd bumped into each other almost as much as they'd hit their target.

The stench of black magic combined with sulfur and brimstone permeated the air around them. Sarah Beth quickly lit the copper pot full of herbs and roots she and her daughters had earlier prepared to dispel any ill effects the noxious fumes may have on them. It took only a few seconds for the witch's brew to dispel the smog, but Drago's still healing eyes burned and watered so badly his limited vision was even blurrier.

"Going to be depending on those dragon senses. You up for the challenge, my friend?" he spoke directly to his beast, who chuffed and pawed the ground in his mind. It was obvious the winged warrior was happy to be part of the fight in any way that he could.

Rayne, Kellan, and Royce took over, kicking the remaining debris from the tunnel to make sure there was ample room for the dragons to protect the McKennons as they entered the last but most densely spelled part of the underground cavern. Kyra and Royce led the way, with Rian and Sarah Bath right behind, closely followed by Drago and Alicia. Had the Assassin had his way, his mate would've been farther back in the line. However, the ladies had decided the order based on magical proficiency, and from the look Alicia gave him when he opened his mouth to protest, the Guardsman decided it was not a battle he was going to win, so shut his mouth and nodded.

The witches were chanting their Banishing Spell as the group cautiously moved through the tunnel, only stopping when every witch and Guardsman was within the cursed cavern. The sigils flamed to life but unlike the others, didn't blink from existence or change colors. These actually bled. Dark, inky gore seeped from the carvings while a low, haunting moan rose from the dirt beneath their feet. The louder the witches chanted, the brighter the sigils glowed. The blood flowed down the walls and across the floor as if it was alive and coming to attack the witches.

Preparing to remove his mate from harm, Drago reached for Alicia just as the witches raised their arms and shouted, *"A bheith imithe Demon!"* in unison while throwing the contents of their sachets at the attacking fluid.

A loud pop and a bright burst of light exploded before them. A blood-curdling scream echoed off the walls and smoke filled the tunnel. Drago was left completely blind. Luckily, he could feel Alicia's elation through their mating bond. He could see in her thoughts this was what Kyra and Sarah Beth had been preparing the McKennons for while he'd been knocking down the wall.

As the smoke cleared and what little sight he had returned, the Assassin could see the blood had been reduced to ashes. The sigils, although not glowing, were still dark black and the presence of black magic still palpable

"A little heads up would have been nice. You could give an old man a heart attack."

"Hold on, it's not over yet," was Alicia's only response before Kyra shouted, *"Ara is go dti' ifreann! Riamh ar ais!"*

The McKennons echoed the tiny witch's spell in unison. The sigils receded into the stone only to burst forth and float in the air above their heads.

"*Solas!*" Sarah Beth commanded just a second before flame lit the candles the witches carried.

Holding the light above their heads, the witches repeated, "*Ara is go dti' ifreann! Riamh ar ais!*"

One last burst of light and the sigils blinked from existence. A sigh of relief filled the cavern as the Guardsmen gave the witches a questioning look. It was Rayne who asked what the others were thinking. "And you couldn't have told us what was going to happen before shaving at least a few years off our lives?"

Kyra moved away from Royce, who was obviously less than happy about what had just happened and was letting his mate know about it in no uncertain terms. "I…We weren't exactly sure how it was going to go down. Sarah Beth and I had a good idea, but nothing with this much evil is ever set in stone, so we played the odds. I knew if y'all had any idea what was going to happen," she looked at Royce and winked, only to be regarded with a growl and a frown, "there was no way you'd let us go through with it. I knew we had the magic we needed, we just had to get in here and do it. Sorry about the scare, but now we can move on."

Shaking his head, the Commander sighed. "I get your motivation, just do *not* agree with your tactics. Let's not do this again, shall we?"

"Yeah, I'm thinking I need new boxers and bottle of hooch," Rory joked, trying to ease the tension.

"There will be further discussion, mate," Royce growled when Kyra returned to his side after nodding to Rayne.

"Whatever, big guy. I got this," Kyra said as she turned her back on him before shouting, "Oh, my Goddess! She's close! I can feel Mom. She's not far from here!"

For several heartbeats no one moved. Drago wasn't even sure if anyone breathed. Then it was as if a switch had been flipped. Kyra looked to Royce and then Rayne. "We have to go! She's hurt."

And with that, she was off and running.

Chapter Fifteen

They caught up to Kyra as she was dumping out her backpack under what appeared to be a trapdoor. Alicia's mom was standing beside the tiny witch as they discussed something that had them both frowning and looking at the door above them. Alicia bent at the waist, placing her hands on her thighs, and tried to catch her breath. Running was not something she enjoyed or did often, if ever. She knew she had more than a few pounds to lose but had decided long ago running would never be her thing.

Drago rubbed her back while having the audacity to not even have broken a sweat. Not able to raise her head, she griped, "I guess I should be glad you didn't throw me over your shoulder again so we could get here faster."

"I thought about it but…"

Whatever Drago was about to say was interrupted by Kyra as she asked for their attention. "I know what I'm about to ask you to do is above and beyond any friendship or kinship we share. It's going to be dangerous. I can only feel my mom, I can't communicate with her. I can tell that she is hurt, but as Royce keeps reminding me, she's a tough old bird and I believe we're here in time.

"Sarah Beth and I are going to scry to see what exactly is up there. I can tell you just from what I can feel that it's a lot of black magic and evil intent. I just need y'all to form a circle and lend us your power. It shouldn't take long."

When the McKennons had formed a sacred circle and Melanie had said the incantation to close it, Kyra and Sarah Beth took the antique silver mirror the tiny witch had covered with salt and rosemary. They lit the white pillar candle symbolizing the Goddess and began to recite the spell that would show them their enemies. In less than five minutes, Alicia could see pictures forming on the glass.

The young witch was too far to see what they were but could see from the look on her mother's face that it was not good news. Kyra gasped then cursed. "Son of a bitch! I will rip the flesh from his hide. That bastard has her chained with iron."

Jumping up, Kyra looked at Royce. "He's torturing her. I have no clue why but the bastard and his flunkies are gathered around a Summoning Circle and that can't be good."

Turning back to Sarah Beth, Kyra shocked everyone by asking, "What's the best way to get up there?"

It was obvious she was too worried about her mother to be making decisions and knew it. Sarah Beth took a few moments to think while everyone else remained silent. Alicia knew her mom hated to be the center of attention and was proud of the way Sarah Beth looked Rayne and Rian each in the eye before answering Kyra. She had acknowledged their positions of authority but needed to speak to the one person with the most at stake.

"I believe if we move fast enough we can use the dragons' magic for cover and our magic to infiltrate. I believe whatever they are up there conjuring has their full attention. Sheer number and the element of surprise will be our advantage, but we need to move quickly. Cleland is impatient. Either he'll get what he wants or he'll move on and most likely take Calysta with him"

Kyra nodded. "I agree." Then turned to her mate who stood beside Rian, Rayne, and Drago. "What do y'all think? Can we make this happen?"

"As if we have a choice. Your mother and I may not be buddies but we never leave one of our own behind," Royce answered, taking Kyra's hand and pulling her to him.

"I'm proof of that," Drago added.

Alicia squeezed his hand, chuckling when he whispered in her mind, *"Your mom's an expert strategist."*

"She had to be with seven magical daughters."

"You are one of us, Kyra. Of course, we're going after Calysta. What do you think we've all been waiting for? Plus, there's not a one of us that doesn't want a piece of Cleland and the *Dorcha*," Rayne confirmed what everyone was thinking.

"There is literally no time to waste," Sarah Beth said, assuming the lead for the witches. "I'm gonna guess that you guys can jump through that trapdoor once we have it open, right? I'm thinking this rickety rope ladder won't hold y'all. No offense, but you know you're huge."

The Guardsmen laughed while nodding as Sarah Beth continued to explain the plan. In no time at all everyone was in place and ready to go. The air was thick with anticipation and tension. Looking from one face to another, Alicia could see the intense focus and dedication each person had to what they were trying to accomplish.

Offering a silent prayer to the Goddess, she watched her mother for the sign to move. A single nod had the witches scurrying up the rope ladder while the Guardsmen stood at the ready to jump through the trapdoor as soon as it was open. The dragons' magic filled the air, dancing on Alicia's skin like little butterflies.

A single word spell uttered by Sarah Beth had the trapdoor popping open just enough for her to slide her fingers under and quietly lift it the rest of the way as she climbed through. Alicia watched her mother and then Kyra disappear into the opening that reeked of sulfur as she hurried up the ladder.

Drago's words floated through her mind. *"Be careful, mo ghra'. I'll be right there."*

Once inside, Alicia was glad to see a makeshift wall of old furniture and debris separating them from the *Dorcha*. She helped the rest of her sisters and Melanie through the door and then they all stood back as one by one, eleven Guardsmen jumped through the trapdoor, immediately forming a wall of muscle between the witches and the *Dorcha*. Alicia breathed a sigh of relief when Drago appeared and took his place with the dragons.

He gave her a quick grin before drawing his broadsword from the sheath on his back and turning toward the stacks of garbage. The others followed suit, assuming a fighting stance. The Dragon Guard was a truly amazing sight at all times, but when they were going into battle, it was spectacular to behold.

In that moment, the young witch knew exactly why *these* men had been chosen. Why their families had been given the honor of carrying the essence of a dragon within them. They were honorable, without reproach, and willing to give their very lives for what they believed in. To know the Universe had chosen her…had made *her,* little ole Alicia May McKennon, to be the mate of a dragon, was staggering and something she decided to think about later as her mother gave the go sign.

Everything happened at once. The Guardsmen burst into the room where Cleland worked his black magic and immediately became engaged in battle with the athame-wielding members of the *Dorcha* who had been lying in wait. Alicia took an extra second to watch the grace with which Drago wielded his blade. It was truly poetry in motion. She was amazed at his accuracy with the condition of his eyes and almost felt pity for the wizard who met the end of his blade.

Bringing her attention back to the matter at hand, Alicia followed the others along the path the Guardsmen were cutting through the *Dorcha*. They avoided the blades and made as direct a path as possible toward Cleland, chanting the spell that would drown the *Draoi's* Summoning Circle in pure white magic. Unfortunately, it bounced off an invisible shield and evaporated into thin air.

Cleland and his followers continued to call to the evil forces, completely ignoring the war erupting around them. Black smoke and soot rose from the portal beneath the blood-drawn pentagram etched into the floor. The longer it took to find a way through the barrier, the closer the *Dorcha* came to raising a demon from the depths of Hell.

With Calysta free and Royce taking her to safety, Kyra joined the McKennons. "Make a circle around theirs," she commanded.

The witches obeyed.

"Say the Banishing Spell and throw the salt," the witch yelled over the growing noise of the combat around them.

As one unit, the witches shouted the spell and threw the salt. It was like water hitting an electrified fence. Sparks flew in every direction. Tiny holes began to form in the magical barrier, allowing their white magic to seep into the portal, causing it to start collapsing.

Cleland leapt from his position at the head of the Summoning Circle. A look of surprise was quickly replaced by hatred as the *Grand Draoi* began issuing orders to the four wizards also in the circle with him. The tall, robed men stood and turned, forming a tight perimeter around the portal to keep the witches' white magic out.

The ten white witches' voices rose until each was shouting the Banishing Spell while pouring all the magic they could into the deep dark hole. Cleland scurried like the rat he was, desperately trying anything possible to keep the white magic at bay until whatever was rising from Hell could arrive.

An agonizing, ear-splitting screech burst forth from the hole in the floor combining with the clash of swords and the witches' chant after an exceptionally powerful wave of white magic made its way through the wizards' defenses. The noise in the room was deafening. Had it not been for her bond with Drago, Alicia would have never known when the *Dorcha's* blade struck his ribs.

Instinctively turning to help her mate, Alicia was pulled into the vacuum created by the collapsing portal. Only the death grip Melanie and Hannah had on her hands kept her from being swept away. Struggling to maintain her footing and make her way out of the deadly suction of black magic, she watched Drago take the head of his opponent before rushing to her aid.

Blood poured from his wound as he grabbed her forearms and pulled. Jace and Liam appeared beside their mates and gripped Alicia's elbows on either side, lending their immense strength to her struggle for freedom. Almost free from the vacuum, the young witch dared to look over her shoulder. Running toward her, athame in one hand and a gris gris bag in the other, Cleland grabbed her outstretched ankle, scratching her with his blade and pulling her back into his web of black magic.

Drago roared. A huge red light emanated from his body as Alicia felt him give control over to his dragon. The glow around her mate took the form of the great beast who was also her mate. A power she could have never imagined flowed between them.

Cleland shrieked as he was pulled farther and farther away from the portal and closer to those who wanted to see him dead. At the last moment, the *Draoi* let go of Alicia's ankle. Momentum pushed her directly into her mate's arms while it flung Cleland backward into his followers.

The five men landed in a pile on the edge of the gateway to Hell. The black smoke thickened. The ear-splitting screech turned to maniacal laughter. Enormous skeletal hands emerged, grabbing the *Draoi* and his followers and dragging them into inky darkness. Blood-curdling screams could be heard as Cleland and the wizards descended into the depths of Hell.

The smoke and soot receded as the portal slowly closed and then blinked out of existence, leaving only a greasy spot where it has once been. Sarah Beth and Kyra immediately began performing a Cleansing Ritual, while Alicia thanked the Goddess that she was alive.

Without so much as a word, Drago carried Alicia toward the hole and jumped down. When they'd reached the spot where her mate's broken coffin lay Alicia was fed up with the silent treatment, so she did the only thing she could think of to get him to stop and put her down… she pinched his arm.

"Ouch! What the hell was that for?" Drago asked, stopping and letting her slide down his body before taking a step back and glaring at her.

"It was to get you to stop and talk to me. I understand if you're upset about what just went down. I have to admit I wasn't thrilled. I was actually scared shitless but dammit, the silent treatment is not cool. You even blocked our bond. Which by the way is not fair, since I don't know how to do that. You have to say *something*. Talk to me. Just *freaking* talk to me!" Alicia was growling by the time she took a breath, which was very unlike her but in her defense, the last few minutes had been incredibly daunting.

Drago stood motionless, his face expressionless, and since he'd blocked their bond, there was absolute silence. It was a true Mexican standoff. Alicia wasn't sure if she should yell some more or keep having the staring contest he'd started. Quickly deciding there was no way in hell she was going to let him win an argument she didn't even understand why they were having, she put her fists on her hips and stared back. It was hard to ignore the blood still seeping from the wound on his side, but it was obvious he was healing so she tried to put it out of her mind.

The sound of approaching footsteps drew her attention. Turning her head to see who was coming, Alicia squeaked her surprise when Drago's arm came around her waist and she found herself thrown over his shoulder, traveling so fast everything was a blur. Only the presence of the cool night air and the smells of the forest let her know they had exited the crater.

In mere seconds her senses were bathed in the fresh salty air of the sea and she knew her mate had taken them to the edge of the cliffs. Forward motion stopped and Alicia found herself unceremoniously, although gently, set upon a large rock overlooking the ocean. Drago paced in front of her, avoiding eye contact and grumbling under his breath.

On his fourth pass, Alicia sighed. On the eighth, she yawned, and on the tenth, she gave up and said, "Oh, my Goddess, get it over with. Yell at me. Scream at me. Do whatever you need to do but stop this…this…whatever the hell this is."

Spinning on his heels, Drago closed the gap between them in three large steps. He leaned down until they were eye to eye with only inches separating them and growled, "You want to know what this is, *ceann beag*? Do you really want to know?"

Nodding because words escaped her, Alicia waited.

"This is a dragon at the end of his rope. I thought I had lost you. I thought Cleland was going to throw you in the pit. In the blink of an eye, I saw my world without you and do you know what it was like?"

She shook her head.

Drago took a deep breath. His eyes closed as he slowly exhaled, his warm breath a kiss against her cheek as Alicia watched her mate struggle for control. When he opened his eyes, it dawned on her that he'd lost his dark lenses during the fight. She'd been so mad before it had escaped her attention. Now she could appreciate the bit of the brown that was returning to his iris whereas before they had been as black as the night sky above them. He no longer growled when he spoke. Instead, she could hear pain and a fear that hadn't even been present when he was locked in that horrid box.

"Desolate. A vast wasteland of nothingness… because there is nothing without you, Alicia. Now that I've tasted life as your mate, I will cease to exist the moment you are no longer by my side. We are two halves of the same whole. Without you, they may as well put me back in that damned box and bury me in the ground, for I will wither and die. You are my reason for being. You are my everything."

Alicia opened her mouth to speak but all she could manage was a sob. Tears flowed from her eyes as she looked at the man she was destined to spend eternity with. Throwing her arms around his neck, she pulled Drago to her. Her Guardsman knelt between her legs as their lips met. Their kiss was passionate and all encompassing. It was a promise of what they meant to each other and the life they would have together. The future both dreamt of. Each opened completely to the other with an understanding that as long as they stood together, no one could tear them apart.

There, under the stars, Alicia truly understood what it meant to mate a dragon and she couldn't have been happier.

Chapter Sixteen

After their night under the stars, Drago had no intention of waiting one second longer than was absolutely necessary to officially make Alicia his mate. The next morning, he got Rian's approval, as well as the okay from the Elder of the Golden Fire Clan, Carrick. His old friend was extremely shocked and incredibly happy that Drago had survived all those years of captivity and wished him congratulations on finding his mate.

Now, twenty-four hours later, the Guardsman known as the Assassin was waiting on the same cliffs that had been his prison for almost a hundred years for the woman of his dreams to arrive. Drago was nervous and excited and more than anything, ready to be officially mated to the woman destined to be his. Rayne and Kyndel had helped him with all the preparations. Tomas and Cole, two young Guardsmen, were escorting Alicia on horseback to the site of their ceremony.

Drago had been up since before dawn making sure every detail was perfect. Alicia's sisters had been a godsend. They decorated everything to his exact specifications and only teased him a little bit the fifth time he was going over his checklist. The entire scene was a wash of bright yellow daffodils setting the air alive with the scent that reminded him of Alicia, and vibrant red roses to signify the unending love he, a red dragon, had for his mate.

Looking out over the ocean on the largest plateau on the entire seaboard, Drago would pledge his love and undying devotion to the woman the Universe created for him and him alone. They would leave here today wearing matching marks of their bond, a bond that would last through the ages.

The sound of horse hooves against stone drew his attention. Ducking behind a large boulder, he watched as Tomas helped Alicia dismount while Cole held the huge bouquet of long-stemmed red roses Drago had placed along the trail for her to find.

The gown Kyndel had helped him design was a perfect fit. The tiny white straps over her shoulders highlighted her peaches and cream complexion and the tiny little freckles that made his mouth water as he imagined tasting each one. He was once again glad to see the advances in women's clothing during his time as a prisoner. The Guardsman was definitely of the opinion that more skin showing was better, especially when he was the one looking.

Any other man will lose his eyes if I catch him so much as glancing at my mate.

The bodice, as the seamstress had called it, was form fitting, perfectly showing off Alicia's curves and ample breasts. Drago worked hard to rein in his libido and reminded both himself and his dragon that they had to make it through the ceremony before they could rip the dress from her body.

He followed her long, flowing skirt to the ground, admiring the fire red flames stitched into the white gossamer fabric. Alicia's toes, painted a bright red, peeked out from under the hem.

She was barefoot, just as the mates from his time always were. It was something he'd thought about but never mentioned.

She must've pulled it from my mind. My little witch never ceases to amaze me.

The young men led Alicia to the white wrought iron chair that had been decorated with daffodils, roses, and ribbons. The white carpet under her chair led to an archway that stood in the middle of the Sacred Circle. Behind the circle was a raised platform holding four large, black, wrought iron chairs closely resembling thrones. Drago knew the Elders of the Blue Thunder Clan, with Rian as their leader, would occupy those chairs very shortly.

He was watching Alicia nervously looking around when Rayne's voice sounded in Drago's mind. *"You ready to do this?"*

"Son, I am as ready as it gets."

"We're heading out. Best of luck."

Drago could only smile while watching Alicia's surprise as Rayne and the other Guardsmen filed out in full-dress uniform. He had earlier explained to her how they wore surcoats in the color of each man's dragon scales, and that there was a dragon in the throes of battle embroidered across the chest, but to see her reaction to seeing them with her own eyes was priceless.

Once the Guardsmen were in place, the Elders immediately took their position on the podium. Drago waited impatiently for Rian to look his way. Finally, he got the nod and strode out, immediately finding Alicia's eyes and holding them hostage. He wanted to experience *everything* with her, beginning right now and lasting forever.

Stopping in front of the dais to the left of the Sacred Circle, Drago stood and waited. He could see impatience and a little uncertainty in Alicia's eyes but sent a wave of calm to her through their mating bond.

Rian stood and began to speak, "Long ago when knights and dragons fought side by side for King and Country, it became apparent that dragon kin was no longer safe from those that would expose and destroy them. They sought to join with the knights that had so valiantly fought alongside them. Thus, through magic and the will of both dragon and knight, the Golden Fire Clan of the Dragon Shifters and the Blue Thunder Clan was born.

"We are here today in this blessed place to honor what the Universe put into motion all those many years ago. We are here to acknowledge and bless the mating of Drago Magnus MacLendon to the one the Universe made for only him, Alicia May McKennon. Will those seeking to witness this union please step forward?"

Drago watched as the nine men he would now call brethren, just as he had their fathers before them, knelt around the Sacred Circle and bowed their heads. He was sad his own Force could not be there and prayed he would soon find them. Rayne and Rory stood and faced the Elders. Rory spoke. "We, the six of the

Aherne Force and our brethren from the MacLendon Force, wish to witness and offer our blessing to the union of these two souls, two halves of the same whole. May they live long, fight hard, love harder, and produce many young to flourish in this world when their souls have gone to the Heavens." Rayne nodded to Rian and then to his uncle and followed Rory back to their men.

Once both were again kneeling with heads bowed, Rian spoke, "Your witness and blessing have been acknowledged and accepted Aherne and MacLendon Forces. Drago MacLendon, you may go to your mate."

Using his enhanced speed, Drago raced to Alicia, took her hands into his, and slowly walked backward, leading her to the Sacred Circle. Rian began again, "The Red Dragons were born of blood and fire. They are notoriously passionate in all areas of their lives. Red Dragons are known for their command and fierceness. The red of their scales symbolizes love and fertility. Red Dragons will lead the charge, conquer the enemy, and defend homeland and family with their very lives. To mate a Red Dragon means to accept all that they are and honor the power shared between mates.

"Now is the time of the marking. May the Universe continue to bless you and yours all the days of your lives." It took only a moment for everyone but Drago and Alicia to leave the plateau, but not before Rayne, Lance, and Royce surrounded the couple with large white screens just as the Assassin had planned. There was no way he was sharing the marking of his mate with a single solitary soul.

Drago stood, awestruck, looking into the eyes of the love of his life. Unable to take the anticipation any longer, Drago lowered his mouth to hers. He stopped right before their lips would have touched and whispered, *"Ta' mo chroi' istigh ionat,"* and with that, he lowered his lips onto hers.

Chapter Seventeen

It was an all-encompassing, devastatingly enraptured kiss. Drago felt his little witch in every cell of his body. The couple was consumed with a passion that threatened to set them ablaze. The Assassin's body and soul laid open to his mate just as he could feel her open to him.

Alicia flinched in his arms at the same time he felt a twinge on the side of his neck. The Universe was marking them as mates. Drago trailed kisses across her jaw and down her neck, reaching the tender spot he knew still stung from their brand. Kissing the offending spot until all thoughts of anything but their naked bodies loving one another were banished from both their minds, Drago knew he'd found true happiness in his little witch.

Lifting his head from her neck, Drago looked at Alicia. He would spend every day of the rest of his life thanking the Universe for her. Kissing the tip of her nose, he looked into her passion-fogged eyes, and whispered, "I need to be alone with you, Alicia. I need to make love to my mate."

Her simple nod was all it took. Lifting her into his arms, Drago used his enhanced speed to get them to the house Rian had given him just the day before. Throwing open the door, the Assassin quickly carried Alicia across the threshold. He needed her naked and in their bed more than he ever needed anything in his life.

Releasing her legs, she slid down his body. The friction of her body against his fed the fire that caused his pulse to race and his cock to harden. Drago held Alicia steady when her toes touched the floor and together, they let out a long, slow breath. They were together in all things. She was his. She bore his mark. There was nothing in Heaven or Hell that could tear them apart. Not even death.

Running his hands through her hair, he released the pins holding her curls. She moaned as he massaged her scalp, pushing her head further into his hands. He rubbed and kneaded down her neck and onto her shoulders, those little freckles teasing him again. This time he did not resist. He kissed each little spot, paying extra attention to the ones one her neck.

Kissing across her décolletage, Drago slid the thin straps from her shoulders and undid the tiny pearl buttons holding the bodice of her dress closed. His breath caught in his throat as her breasts came into view. Undoing the last pearl, the Guardsman let go of the material and her gown floated to the ground. Alicia lifted one foot and then the other as Drago kicked the garment out of their way. He took a moment just to marvel at the miraculous creature standing before him in nothing but white lace panties.

Oh yeah, women's clothing is so much better now.

"It seems, Mr. MacLendon, that you are a tad overdressed." Alicia batted her eyes as she lifted his surcoat over his head and reached for the hem of his black undershirt.

Drago wrapped his hands around hers and held them tight, but Alicia shook her head. "Let me return the favor," she said, and then winked at him through her thick, dark lashes.

His hands fell to his sides. The infamous Dragon Guard Assassin stood in awe of his beautiful mate. She made quick work of his undershirt and ran her hands over his shoulders and across his chest. Rubbing along each ridge of his six-pack, Alicia made her way to the thin line of hair leading into the waistband of his pants. Drago thought he might lose his mind as she undid the clasp and zipper of his pants, running the back of her fingers from one hip to the other. Drago shivered at the sensation.

Pushing his pants off his hips, she followed them to the floor and sat on her knees in front of him, his erection right in front of her mouth. Alicia licked her lips, capturing the small bead of moisture at the tip of his cock with the end of her tongue. Drago knew without a doubt that the image was forever burned into his memory.

When Alicia started to take him in her mouth, his eyes shot open and he grabbed her shoulders to bring her to her feet. His little witch resisted his touch, looking up in confusion then assuring him, "No, Drago, I *want* to taste you."

Their eyes remained locked. He had to know this was truly what she wanted. The love he saw in her eyes, combined with her tiny nod, had Drago relaxing once again. Alicia placed her palms on his thighs. Her tongue lavished the vein that ran his length, working her way to the tip, then pulling the swollen head into her mouth. When she dipped her tongue into the slit at the very tip, the muscles in his thighs shook. Drago was sure his head would explode if he didn't fall flat on his ass first.

Alicia sucked as much of his length into her mouth as would fit and hollowed her cheeks. Drago's fingers squeezed her shoulders as he groaned. "*Ceann beag*, I have waited a hundred years for you but I won't last another second if you keep doing that."

He felt her smile around his cock. It seemed to spur her on. Alicia worked him in and out of her lips for a few more strokes. He grew larger and thicker, working hard not to explode in her mouth. Moving back to the tip, she increased the suction and pulled him from her mouth. Quicker that he could track, she sucked one and then the other of his balls into her mouth, licking and massaging with her tongue until he was no longer light-headed.

But his little witch was not about to let him rest. Alicia took his length in her mouth again. Placing both her hands around the base, she worked him in and out of her mouth, sucking and humming until he was helpless to anything but release into her beautiful mouth. His mate swallowed all he gave, kissing up and down his length until he began to harden again.

It was wonderful torture but his turn to taste had come. Putting his hands under her arms, he used his enhanced speed to get her on her back in the middle of his bed. One more move and her legs were over his shoulders. Drago smiled as he rubbed his nose against the wet silk of her panties, inhaling the scent of daffodils and warm sunshine. The Guardsman knew if he didn't taste his little witch in the next few seconds he might die.

Slipping two fingers under the silk at her hip, Drago ripped the offending material and threw it over his head. No longer able to stand the torture, the tip of his tongue licked up and down the glistening seam of her pussy.

Drago groaned deep in his throat as her taste burst upon his tongue. Unable to wait one second longer to taste deep inside her, he placed his hands under her ass, lifted her pussy closer to his face, and began to feast. Driving his tongue in her warm, wet pussy as far as he could go, the Assassin licked every inch of his little witch, curling the end of his tongue to tease her sensitive bundle of nerves.

Alicia's hands grabbed his hair, pulling with such force he was sure he would be bald. His mate gasped for breath and Drago smiled against her skin just knowing how much he excited her.

Using the flat of his tongue, he licked her outer lips from bottom to top, teasing her clit with tiny circles on every pass. Her legs tightened around his head while her heels dug into his back. She moaned to the Heavens as he sucked her swollen nub between his lips, flicking it up and down with his tongue until Alicia was screaming her release to the Goddess above.

Drago continued to drink the honey that flowed from her. He nuzzled and nipped her puffy lips until she released his hair and her breathing returned to normal. Carefully lifting her legs off his shoulders, he massaged her thighs. There had never been a lovelier sight than his little witch completely satisfied from his attention, looking like the Goddess Athena in his bed.

He kissed her hip and then her belly button, where he paid extra attention with his tongue until Alicia started to giggle. He then nipped his way up her stomach to the sweet spot between her breasts, feeling her heart beat in sync with his. Palming both her breasts, Drago gently squeezed as the already raised peaks grew harder against his palms. Kissing up her neck, he paid special attention to the triple flames marking her neck. His mark that he would never tire of seeing on her skin. Kissing her neck, Alicia sighed and moved her head to the side, allowing him greater access.

His little witch surprised him by grabbing his head and kissing him with wild abandon. Drago opened immediately, letting Alicia have her way with him. His mate was sassy in bed and in love. He couldn't have asked for any more. Her hands in his hair and her tongue working his mouth had him ready to explode again. He shifted his hips slightly, pushing into her until he could go no farther. He knew he'd done as she wished when she tore her mouth from his, screaming, "Drago! Yes! Oh, my Goddess, yes! I love you!"

He wanted to go slow this first time in her body, but the feel of her muscles contracting around his extremely hard cock made it impossible for him to hold still. Sliding out of her until only the tip of him rested within her opening, he whispered into her mind,

"Look at me, Alicia. I need to see your eyes as we truly become one."

Her eyes snapped to his. The Assassin was floored by the love overflowing from his mate. He thrust into her and pulled right back out, starting a rhythm that Alicia met stroke for stroke. Staring into one another's eyes, their passion exploded. He pushed her knees toward her chest, lifting her bottom off the bed, allowing him deeper access to her wet, wanting pussy. Rolling his hips, the head of his cock caressed the sensitive bundle of nerves that made the walls of her vagina close tighter around him. He wanted to shout to the Heavens when her eyes rolled back in her head from sheer pleasure. He watched her struggle to breathe, just as he also had trouble drawing his next breath.

Drago reached between their bodies, barely touching her clit with his thumb before Alicia's orgasm overtook them both. Her mouth opened in a silent scream. Her brilliant blue eyes holding all the promise of their future locked on his and he was helpless but to follow her over the edge. The Guardsman knew he would follow his little witch anywhere, even to the end of the earth.

Hours later they lay completely satiated, her head on his chest, their legs intertwined, while their bodies cooled from their hours of lovemaking. Drago reached under his pillow and pulled out a red, silk pouch. He placed it in the hand she had laying on his chest.

Alicia sat up, furrowed her brow, and asked, "What's this?"

"Open it and see."

Tipping the pouch, Alicia gasped when the ring that had been his mother's fell into her hand.

"What the... no way. This is too much."

"It is not too much. It is yours and I will not rest until it is on your finger."

"But, Drago...

"But nothing. It was my mother's and Rayne had kept it all these years after Alexander told him it was meant to be my mate's."

"But it is just…"

"It is just yours. Now, let me put it on your finger."

Not waiting for Alicia's response, Drago took her left hand in his and slid the ring on her ring finger. After a moment of admiring what had been in his family for generations, he explained its significance. "This ring has been worn by the mate of the eldest son of the Clan MacLendon since our beginning. The ruby in the center signifies the blood we shed for our own. The diamonds surrounding it stand for the original eight clans that came together to form Clan MacLendon even before we were dragon shifters. The black sapphire at the top is for the wisdom of our people and the protection of body and soul we offer our mates."

When he looked up, Alicia was crying, but this time he understood they were happy tears and only smiled when she cuddled against his chest. It took a few minutes for his little witch to regain control but when she did, she sat back and looked him in the eyes. "Thank you so much, Drago. I love you more than all the stars in the sky."

"What did you say?" he asked, sure he'd misunderstood.

"I said I love more than all the stars in the sky. To be honest, I've never said it before. It just popped into my mind and it seemed to fit, so I said it."

Throwing his head back and laughing aloud, it took Drago a minute before he could explain, and when he did, his little witch laughed right along with him.

"So you see, *mo ghra'*, that is what my mother used to say to my father every time he went into battle. As a little boy I used to sit by the window and watch him ride out of our lair, waiting for the day my mate would say the same thing to me."

He paused as his love for his incredible mate overflowed. Unable to finish out loud, Drago spoke into Alicia's mind. *"You,* mo maite, *have made all my dreams come true."*

"Drago?"

"Yes, mo ghra'*?"*

"I still want to meet your dragon in person."

Chuckling at his amazing mate, Drago simply answered, *"You wish is my command…later."*

Epilogue

Tomas has been summoned by none other than Rayne MacLendon, the Commander of his Force, and the one man in all the world the young Guardsman thought of as a role model. Tomas had been training with Rory, the Commander of the Blue Thunder Force, when Rayne had called to him through their unique link. As always, the Commander was a man of few words, only saying, *"Tomas, come to my home. See you in ten."*

The whole way there Tomas replayed the last week in his mind. He knew everything had been quiet since Rayne's uncle, Drago, had mated Alicia McKennon. The weeks leading up to their mating had been nuts but since then nothing, nada, zip, zilch. The young guardsman had even done extra training sessions and missed out on the party one of his brethren had thrown in the woods. So when he knocked on Rayne's door, he was clueless as to why he'd been called.

Kyndel, the Commander's mate, answered the door with smile on her face and their son on her hip. "Come on, Rayne is out back. Grab something to drink on your way through the kitchen. I have to put Jay down for his nap."

Tomas walked out onto the patio and waited for Rayne to acknowledge his presence, just as his training dictated. His wait was short as the Commander spoke over his shoulder, "This is an informal request, Tomas. Come on up here and let's talk."

Unsure how to act, the young guardsman did as he had been instructed. Several tense minutes passed before Rayne turned to him with a furrowed brow and began speaking. "I have a favor to ask. Not as your Commander but as a fellow Guardsman. It is a big one and please feel free to say no if you don't feel comfortable with my request."

Tomas nodded.

Rayne went on, "You know that we found a focus stone along with my uncle, right?"

"Yes, sir."

"Yes, sir? What's with the formalities?" Royce teased as he walked out onto patio.

"It's a sign of respect. Something you should also be showing me," Rayne joked before adding, "I was just about to ask him. You're early."

Tomas' intuition said whatever was happening was important and not something he should take lightly. His suspicions were confirmed when Rayne turned back to him. "Okay, where were we? Oh yes, the focus stone. Anyway, no one here, not even Calysta or Kyra know what this thing is. We all know it holds power but other than that, it's a total mystery, and no matter what anyone tries, they can't purify. The worst part is it seems to be gaining strength and we have no clue if its magic is white or black. It appears to flip flop, depending on who's around it. Needless to say, it needs to be studied. There is an Elder, the oldest of our kin, who has the power and knowledge to study it. His name is Maddox and he lives in the North Country."

The Commander paused, looked at Royce, shook his head, and went on, "I hate to ask this of you, but I need you to take the stone to Maddox. I would do it but I have to get Kyndel and Jay back to our lair for Christmas. Lance and Devon have already left so that Siobhan can be in her own home for the holiday and they can be with their mates. Royce has to stay with Kyra while Calysta is convalescing and to be honest, I want it to be one of my clan that delivers it to the Elder, not a blue dragon. I just have a feeling it's our responsibility. I know it's a lot to ask but if you leave today, you should be able to be back at our lair in time for Christmas dinner. Whatcha say, Tomas, will you do this for me?"

There was never a question in the young Guardsman's mind. Of course, he would do whatever Rayne MacLendon asked of him. Without hesitation, Tomas nodded. "Absolutely, sir."

Royce chuckled behind him. "Again with the sir. Boy, you're gonna give the Commander here a big head."

"Shut up, Royce," Rayne growled over Tomas' head before looking him in the eyes. "Thank you very much. I owe you, big time. Now go in the house and Kyra will give you the instructions on handling the stone. She also has the coordinates of Maddox's lair. He's sort of a lone dragon, one of a kind."

Tomas got his instructions from Royce's tiny mate, packed his duffle, called forth his dragon, and took to the sky, remembering what his Commander had said…

"…if you leave today, you should be able to be back at our lair in time for Christmas dinner."

Sounds good. What could go wrong?

~~*~*~*~*~*

Calysta was tired of lying in bed, tired of feeling like an invalid, and really tired of her sister, Della, and Kyra fussing over her every minute of every day. The Grand Priestess knew she'd been through a serious ordeal. Hell, she was the *one* that had gone through it. And after all she'd endured they treated her like a china doll. No one would talk about it in front of her. They all acted like she might break apart if they mentioned Cleland or the *Dorcha* or Goddess forbid, Thanatos.

Sighing to herself, she slowly got out bed, thanking the Universe for her enhanced healing but cursing that even a week and half of lying around she still ached from the iron that had yet to leave her system. One thing was for sure, Cleland knew how to inflict pain on a witch. He was one son of a bitch she'd been glad to hear made his way to Hell before he died. Unfortunately, if the dreams she was having were any indication of what he'd done before his demise, they were all in serious trouble.

The Grand Priestess thought about her last nightmare, trying to see something, anything she'd missed before. The images played back in her mind. She saw the young girl, Mara, who had slipped Cleland's mind control and was actually trying to help Calysta before the girl just disappeared.

In her dream, the young witch was walking through the forest. The ground beneath her feet turned brown with each step. Every plant and tree withered as she passed. The birds and animals, even the insects scurried out of her path, literally running for their lives.

Reaching a clearing Calysta didn't remembering ever seeing in her waking hours, but that somehow felt familiar, Mara walked around the perimeter, leaving a scorched circle in her path. As she returned to the spot where she began, the young witch, uttered, *"Se'alaithe,"* closing the circle she'd created.

Sitting on the ground at what Calysta could see was the top of her circle, Mara looked up, as if she somehow knew the Grand Priestess was watching, and in a low, otherworldly voice whispered, "All hail, Thanatos, Death incarnate. We wait your arrival."

Mara eyes turned from their once sparkling cornflower blue to a smoky gray right before she smiled an evil smile and began to chant. What Calysta heard made her blood run cold and sweat roll down her back. The young witch was reciting the words to the spell that would bring Thanatos to the earth. It simply wasn't possible. The spell was hidden at the coven and only one other person other than the Grand Priestess knew where it was and she was without reproach…or was she?

Coming December 1, 2015 as part of the Alphas Unwrapped Anthology

And as a Stand Alone Novel on December 18, 2015

"Her Dragon's No Angel"

Take one snowbound dragon, combine with one Christmas Angel, throw in a healthy dose of an attraction only the Universe could have conjured and top with the largest blizzard in a hundred years.

Now sit back and enjoy the show! This one's gonna be a bumpy ride!

Fate Will Not Be Denied but Heaven's Got a Plan of Its Own!

Here's also an excerpt from

Vidalia: A 'Not-Quite' Vampire Love Story

From Julia's 'Not-Quite' Love Story Series

"Morning, Vi."

"Hey Reggie. What we got?"

"Same as the others. Only looks like this one might've gotten a piece of her attacker."

My assistant, Reggie, pointed to what appeared to be a swatch of fabric still clutched in the victim's hand. Hopefully, she'd also scratched the scumbag who'd thrown her off the balcony of her thirtieth floor penthouse. With any luck, we'd be able to get some DNA and put the person who was doing this behind bars. I know it was a long shot. Up until now, there hasn't even been a speck of dust outta place at any of the crimes scenes, let alone any usable evidence. Finding something was a shot in the dark, but it was the only shot we had.

Dealing with the sixth homicide in as many days, all with the same MO., (jugular *and* carotid cut, drained of all blood then thrown off a high rise building into a busy intersection) was frustrating to say the least. The part both my office and the Police Department were keeping to ourselves was the fact that each vic also sported the letter 'V' carved into a very intimate part of their body. This marking was undetectable by anyone but their mother, their lover, their gynecologist, or in this case, the Medical Examiner. And… that would be me, Vidalia Fitzsimmons.

There are three things you need to know about me before we go any farther. I'm the heiress to the Fitzsimmons' Vidalia onion empire and as southern as the day is long. (Now, you get the name, right?) I'll be thirty in less than two months, my curves have curves, I'm in love with the man of my dreams, and I have great hair (not conceited, just honest. Put away the claws). And…

I'm a vampire. (Not the biting kind. The cursed kind.) Any questions?

Before you go thinking too hard, let me answer the number one question I've been asked my whole life. Why did one of the richest men in Georgia with a pedigree that rivaled British royalty and a wife that was not only a trophy, but also the love of his life, name his only child, Vidalia? It's simple. My daddy only ever truly loved three things: me, Momma, and his onions…Vidalia, Viviana, and Vidalia. It's a Southern thing, just go with it.

Number two question: why is a pretty socialite like me a Medical Examiner? Well, you see, this is easier for y'all to grasp than those that don't *really know* me. Suffice it to say I don't go around flashing my "V Card" to everyone (vampire, not virgin…keep up). I may not be the 'bite first, ask questions later' type of vamp, but I am still a vamp, and that means blood is food. But here's the kicker…it's gotta be 'live' blood. So in the morgue, with *my* patients, I'm good. I became a vampire *after* I became a doctor and wasn't willing to give up my passion, hence Medical Examiner.

This leads me to another important fact you need to know about me. I have no fangs. I know you're thinking that isn't possible, fangs are essential to a vamp. You might even be thinking, 'she's just bat-shit crazy', and let me tell you there are days I think you might be right, but today isn't one of them.

About Julia

Julia Mills is the New York Times and USA Today Bestselling Author of the Dragon Guard Series. She admits to being a sarcastic, southern woman that would rather spend all day laughing than a minute crying. She has two of the most amazing daughters ever created, a menagerie of animals and a voracious appetite for reading. She decided to write the stories running through her brain and is having an absolute blast!! She read her first book, Dr Suess' Cat in The Hat and has been hooked ever since.

She believes a good book along with shoes, makeup and purses will never let a girl down. She knows for a fact that all heroes in all the books she has ever read or will ever write pale in comparison to her hero, her dad! She's a sucker for a happy ending and loves some hot sweaty sex with a healthy dose of romance.

She's still working on her story but can guarantee you that it'll contain as love and laughter as she can cram into it!!!!! Dare to Dream! Have the Strength to Try EVERYTHING! Never Look Back!

Julia absolutely adores stalkers so look her up on Facebook at https://www.facebook.com/JLakeMills?ref=hl and sign up for her newsletter at JuliaMillsAuthor.com.